So here she was.

A nice, square woman, who ....
dead husband's secret novel and a corpse. Ruth Budge
looked down at her hands to see if there were any telltale
marks of her strange activities. The entry door popped
opened and Maude Stone billowed through, her bun
bobbing along behind her.

"He did it again!" she bellowed to no one in particular.
"He does it on purpose. I want him arrested immediately."
She was a tiny woman with a voice intended for a much
larger vessel.

Officer Katz glanced up, covering the phone still
stuck to his ear. "Good morning, Maude. Is that fog
lifting any yet?"

Her eyes widened into saucers and a flush mottled
her face. "I do not want to discuss the weather, Nathan
Katz. I want you to arrest Alva Hernandez this minute."

Don't miss out on a single one of our great mysteries. Contact us at the following address for information on our newest releases and club information:

Heartsong Presents—MYSTERIES! Readers' Service
PO Box 721
Uhrichsville, OH 44683
Web site: www.heartsongmysteries.com

Or for faster action, call 1-740-922-7280.

Trouble Up
Finny's Nose

A Finny's Nose Mystery

Dana Mentink

HEARTSONG
PRESENTS
MYSTERIES

To Him, for giving me wings.
To my Mike, for believing I could fly.
To Susan Downs, for giving me a chance to try.

ISBN 978-1-59789-507-1

Copyright © 2008 by Dana Mentink. All rights reserved. Except for use in any review, the reproduction or utilization of this work in whole or in part in any form by any electronic, mechanical, or other means, now known or hereafter invented, is forbidden without the permission of Heartsong Presents—MYSTERIES, an imprint of Barbour Publishing, Inc., PO Box 721, Uhrichsville, OH 44683.

Scripture taken from the HOLY BIBLE, NEW INTERNATIONAL VERSION®. NIV®. Copyright © 1973, 1978, 1984 by Inter-national Bible Society. Used by permission of Zondervan. All rights reserved.

All of the characters and events in this book are fictitious. Any resemblance to actual persons, living or dead, or to actual events is purely coincidental.

Cover design: Kirk DouPonce, DogEared Design

Our mission is to publish and distribute inspirational products offering exceptional value and biblical encouragement to the masses.

Printed in the U.S.A.

We grow accustomed to the Dark—
When Light is put away—
As when the Neighbor holds the Lamp
To witness her Good-bye
—Emily Dickinson

Prologue

The view from up Finny's Nose was amazing. Breathtaking even. According to the guidebooks, it offered an "uninterrupted panoramic of the majestic Pacific Ocean and its pristine coastline."

Frederick Finny had admired the coastline for a different reason. While aiming for a secluded nook in which to unload his Canadian rum for the parched victims of Prohibition, he ran aground in the treacherous California riptide. The only hope of escape for his vessel was to empty hundreds of barrels of premium liquor into the ocean.

But even after every precious drop was dribbled into salty oblivion, the vessel remained stubbornly wedged. The ship was lost, but Finny old-timers elevated to legend the exploits of a gaggle of drunken crabs that wove their way to the beach and marched in dizzy circles for hours.

Finny slogged ashore and made the best of his misfortune, changing careers from rum smuggling to beekeeping, eventually settling at the top of the steep bluff that looked, for all the world, like a tremendous nose.

In the afternoon sun, through squinted eyes, the town of Finny was straight out of a postcard. The residents and buildings alike seemed to age gently into a condition just shy of shabby with enough quaintness sprinkled throughout to make the town a charming little stop for tourists looking for that perfect coastal escape. Not the overnight, weekend getaway, but more along the lines of a lazy morning stop on the way to the larger towns like Carmel and Monterey—places less shabby and more chic.

On this day, except for the peeling paint on the Finny Hotel and the dead man propped on his head in the Central Park fountain, the town was definitely postcard material.

Alva Hernandez walked his entire route along the foggy main street before he finally stopped to chat with the upside-down man in the fountain. Eventually, he put down his remaining newspapers and whacked on one of the protruding muddy boots. Scratching his grizzled hair, Alva removed his teeth, inserted a lemon drop, and sat down to await further developments.

W hat is this?" Ruth Budge stammered. "What is going on here?" Her husband, Phillip, was supposed to be writing memoirs before his sudden death, a collection of stories from the life of a country vet. What in the world was this thing? Certainly not a recounting of anything her husband had ever experienced. It couldn't be. Ruth began to read again at page one. . .for the third time.

"Oh no!"

She slammed on the brakes and skidded to a stop inches from the squad car. "I get a parking ticket for an expired meter, and this guy can park his cruiser practically in the middle of. . ." Her words trailed off as she noticed the cowboy boot sticking out from under the open car door. "Ohhh. This is not good." Ignoring the pinging of the keys-in-the-ignition warning, she slid out of the car.

The cop was facedown in the gravel, one arm stretched toward the radio, which rested just out of his reach in the dust.

"Are you all right?"

Really smart question, Ben. People commonly lie facedown on the road if they are fit and perky. Especially cops. *Trembling, she knelt down and patted his shoulder.*

"Ummmm. . .sir? Officer? Can you hear me?" She patted some more. With shaking fingers she felt for a pulse under the prickly brown hair just below his throat, recoiling at the stickiness left on her fingertips.

"Ohhh boy. Calm down. Think what to do. Get your cell . . .no!" The phone sat on her kitchen table, recharging.

"*Think! People used to do charitable deeds before cell phones. Okay. Radio.*"

As she fumbled in the gravel for the receiver, a mustard-colored sedan pulled out of the copse of trees and began backing up. Stopping about fifteen yards from where she crouched, three men got out.

She felt her body go cold as she struggled to breathe. Frantically, she pounded the prone figure on the back. "*Please wake up, Mr. Officer. I think this is what you would call a situation.*"

She squeezed the button on the radio. In a cracking sotto voce *tone* she quavered, "*Help me, please! I am Benjamina Pena. I am with, er, a really big cop, and he's unconscious. There are three nasty-looking men on Old Highway One just past the breakwater. I think they're gonna kill us. Ten-four, uh, over and out, oh no!*"

Praying her message had been received by someone— a truck driver, crop duster, anyone—she peeked over the top of the driver's side door. The three men had slowed to a stop a few cautious yards from the car, peering into the windshield and under the front license plate.

"*Hey, lady. What you doin' to that cop? He ain't no business of yours.*"

Desperately, she fumbled with the fastener on his gun belt. "*Yeah? Well, I don't reckon he's any business of yours, either.*" That sounded pretty close to the John Wayne movies she'd seen.

They laughed. One said, "*She has a streak of somethin', eh? We goin' to have fun with you.*"

With a jerk, the catch finally gave way. She yanked the gun out and stood up so quickly it made her dizzy.

"*Okay. Now you listen up, you troglodytes. Any one of you comes a step closer and I'll drop you right where you stand.*"

That brought them up short. After a second of shocked silence, they relaxed. "A trogla-what?" said the skinniest one.

The tallest one with the bandanna tied like a sausage casing around his head interrupted the laughter. "Well, well. Ain't she a tough girly. I guess we got ourselves here a Jane Wayne."

Their eyes widened as she released the safety on the semiautomatic.

Aiming at what she took to be their midsections, midway between the bandannas and underwear poking out of oversized pants, she croaked, "I don't know what your problem is with this cop, but I will shoot you if you take one more step."

Later she tried to recall if they had actually stepped or just realigned their slouching, but somehow she pulled the trigger. The recoil knocked her over, slamming her shoulders into the gravel.

Lying on her back, shoving the hair out of her eyes, she watched the thin man grab his ear and howl in pain. The others hoisted him by the pants and hauled him up the road to their car. They roared away in a shower of loose gravel.

Benjamina watched the dust settle.

She flopped back onto the gravel. "I can't believe I just did that."

⌐—

Ruth rolled the papers into a tube, clutching them to her breast. This story, this novel, whatever it was, had hit her blindside.

She had discovered the small pile of papers in the file drawer, next to the information on her funeral plot. The bizarre surprise threw her completely off balance, compelling her to read and reread before tearing the file cabinet to pieces looking for more. By the time she returned to what was left of her senses, she had missed her morning hair appointment by an hour.

By now, Felice was boarding a plane to Fiji. Ruth felt like crying.

It was not just a matter of vanity. Ruth was not, nor ever had been in her forty-six years of living, a beautiful woman. Nevertheless, she refused to be wandering around town looking like Miss Havisham. When Phillip was alive, he made a point of taking her to lunch after her monthly salon appointments.

"You look like a million bucks," he would say. Her cheeks would warm every time.

Rescheduling with another hairdresser was simply out of the question. Ruth would die with numerous sins on her conscience, but committing infidelity to her long-time hairdresser was not one of them. She would just have to endure the three weeks until Felice returned.

The striking of the clock made her start. She felt guilty, as if she had been caught reading a teenager's diary. "Oh, for goodness' sake," she muttered. "It's not like he'll catch me reading it."

Phillip had been gone for almost two years, and she still expected to see him around every corner like the Ghost of Christmas Past.

She stuffed the papers back into the crammed file drawer and sat in the chair, listening to nothing. There was only a faint rustling from her flock of handicapped seagulls and terns outside and the ticking of the clock inside to break the silence. Ruth looked around the space she had lived in for twenty years and wondered why the furnishings seemed strange to her, as if she were an insect that had just flown through the window to reconnoiter. She folded her hands to pray. "Dear God," she began. After a minute more of silence, she gave voice to the thought that grieved her most. "Where are You?" There was no answer, only that endless tick.

She looked down to see what she had put on in the middle of the night when she mistook it for morning. Faded denim stretch pants and a ragged crocheted sweater the color of a rusty scouring pad. Now that it really was Monday morning, she felt as though she hadn't slept at all the night before. She sat as the silence squeezed in on her with the inexorable pressure of a glacier, until she couldn't stand it any longer. After a quick check of her backyard gaggle, she set off.

The cold morning air left her breathless as she crested the bridge of Finny's Nose. She figured it was an enterprising sweatshirt manufacturer who spread the rumor that California was one warm sandy beach from Canada to Mexico. Though the drive along the rugged coastal cliffs bordering Highway 1 provided spectacular views of secluded beaches, the sun had to wait until the fog evaporated to make an appearance. She had sold many a photo of this amazing scenery to travel magazines. It was quaint, poetic even, and colder than a well-digger's toes. All in all, it was the kind of sleepy little town that fine postcards are made of. The kind of place that, at one time, spoke to Ruth's soul. As she plodded along, her mind replayed scenes from her late husband's. . .novel.

Lost in her own thoughts, she murmured a hello to Alva Hernandez seated on the edge of the Central Park fountain and passed by. Then it hit her. A quick double take dispelled the notion that she was hallucinating. There was definitely a pair of ragged boots protruding from behind Alva's shoulder. A few moments of closer examination convinced her that she wouldn't need her rusty CPR skills.

"Alva. Are you. . .all right?" she asked.

"Yep," he said around a mouthful of yellow candy.

"Oh. Good." She fiddled with the zipper on her jacket. "You know there is a man in the fountain, don't you?"

"Sure do." He stuck a finger deep between cheek and gum to dislodge a sticky ball.

"Well, he—he doesn't seem to be all right," she proposed gently.

"Nope. Ain't moved a bit. Never seen anyone hold their breath that long."

Marveling at the sheer ludicrousness of the situation, she suggested to Alva that perhaps they should have a go at removing the upside-down man from the lazily bubbling water.

"Sure thing. I'll get the starboard side," Alva said cheerfully.

It was as if she were watching from outside herself as they each grabbed a handful of the slippery figure. The man was heavy and uncooperatively stiff. Fighting the bile rising in her throat, Ruth clasped the slick boots, and with Alva tugging vigorously on the man's overalls, the pair hauled the body onto the grass.

The dead face seemed surprised to be looking up into the two live ones. He was cold and slimy, like celery left too long in the vegetable crisper. Ruth leaned back on her heels, nauseous, and then noticed several people hastily making their way over to the damp trio. A few chilled tourists clapped their hands over their mouths in astonishment. The slippery dead man was definitely not part of their mental postcards.

"Ewwww," cried a woman in an *I Went up Finny's Nose* sweatshirt. "Is he really dead?"

"Yep," said Alva. "Pretty much."

By this time, Bubby Dean had emerged from the nearby High Water Pub and ducked his head back inside to call for help. The small crowd grew. Two middle-aged women stood with their hands fluttering over their mouths. A well-dressed man with a speckled bald head talked on a cell phone.

Ruth sat down on the edge of the fountain, suddenly overwhelmed by the outrageous events of the day. The novel. The man in the fountain. Felice in Fiji.

Alva patted her head and said gently, "It's okay, chickie. I got somethin' here for you." He fished around in his pocket and handed her a sucker. It looked as if it had been licked a few times and rewrapped.

The police arrived to find a huddle of tourists, a sticky old man asking bystanders for change, and a middle-aged Ruth Budge, laughing until the tears ran down her chin.

She passed a solitary half hour reading and rereading the posters on the police station wall later that morning. Officer Katz sat behind his desk, chin resting on his hand while he waited patiently for someone on the phone. He'd been holding for ten minutes so far.

Her head whirled at the bizarre turn her life had taken in the past twenty-four hours. Ruth Marylyn Budge was not the sort of person who happened upon secrets and found dead bodies languishing about. Excitement did not visit her often, maybe not ever, except that day in December when a deer found its way into her upstairs bathtub and destroyed two chairs and her hair dryer during its crazed rampage. Her reflection in the mirrored door reminded her that she was basically square—rectangular actually—with a wide brace of collarbones, a thick middle, and short serviceable legs. Solid, reliable, built from sturdy farm stock.

So here she was. A nice, square woman who had recently discovered a dead husband's secret novel and a corpse. She looked down at her hands to see if there were any telltale marks of her strange activities. The entry door popped opened and Maude Stone billowed through, her bun bobbing along behind her.

"He did it again!" she bellowed to no one in particular. "He does it on purpose. I want him arrested immediately." She was a tiny woman with a voice intended for a much larger vessel.

Officer Katz glanced up, covering the phone still stuck to his ear. "Good morning, Maude. Is that fog lifting any yet?"

Her eyes widened into saucers and a flush mottled her face. "I do not want to discuss the weather, Nathan Katz. I want you to arrest Alva this minute."

Nate cleared his throat. "I've told you before, Maude, we can't arrest someone for accidentally stepping on your primroses."

"Accidentally! He does it on purpose. He brings my paper to the door and intentionally ruins my flowers."

Maude lived in the second house down on Whist Street, and the children nicknamed her the Wicked Witch of Whist. Often, on her way to the beach in the wee hours of the morning, Ruth witnessed Alva delivering Maude's paper and zestfully treading on each and every flower with precision.

"Well, I am not going to let you ignore me, Officer." With that, she hiked herself onto his desk and folded her arms defiantly across her striped sweater, like the King of Siam. "I am going to stay right here until you deliver some justice."

In her youth, Maude had been a contortionist in a traveling circus, so it did not surprise Ruth that she made the jump onto Officer Katz's desktop without even rustling his Post-it notes. It didn't seem to surprise the officer, either.

At that moment Nate's colleague Mary Derisi came into the office. She shot a look at the woman standing on Nate's desk. "Hi, Maude. Hi, Ruth. Nate, if you don't stop borrowing my stapler, I will be forced to glue it to my desk."

"Sorry," Nate said, reaching around Maude and handing Mary the stapler.

"So, Ruth," Mary said, flipping her short braid behind her shoulder, "I hear you had quite an experience at the fountain. How are you doing with all that?"

"Oh, well, okay, I guess."

"Good. The weird thing about dead bodies is they look so lifelike, apart from the not breathing thing." She tapped the stapler against her muscular thigh thoughtfully. "Jack is ready to see you now. I'll walk you back." She left the room without a backward glance at the woman atop the desk.

Officer Katz was still holding.

"Do you see this?" Maude yelled to Ruth. "Do you see how these people treat me?"

Ruth nodded, making a mental note to bake some cookies for Nate and Mary before her next hair appointment.

The door to Detective Denny's office opened and Alva shuffled out, a crumpled bag of M&M's in his hand. "Your turn, chickie," he croaked.

"Thank you, Alva. Do you need a ride?"

The detective spoke up. "Officer Katz will be escorting him home."

"On a motorcycle?" Alva's bushy brows zinged upward hopefully as Nate walked up behind Ruth.

"Sorry, Alva. We don't have any motorcycle cops in this department. The car is nice, though. You'll have a comfortable ride." He tried hard to hold the corners of his mouth steady. "Thank you for your time. We'll call if we need any more information."

"Right." Alva hitched up his pants and whispered to Officer Katz. "Is that crazy woman still standing on your desk?"

The officer nodded mournfully.

"She's like a fungus between your toes. You'll never get rid of her." He patted Nate on the back. "Got any change for the candy machine?"

Ruth and the detective watched him depart and settled into the mud-brown office. She noticed a neat circle of yellow M&M's on the mammoth metal desk.

"He doesn't eat the yellow ones?" she asked.

"Nope. Says they taste like, er, urine." They both chuckled. "Hello, Mrs. Budge. It has been a long time, hasn't it?"

"Please call me Ruth. Yes, we haven't spoken in quite a while. If it's all right to ask, how is your little boy?" She watched the pain settle over his handsome face like a fine dust.

"About the same." The wrinkles around his brown eyes were deep. "I forgot how long it's been since we talked last. Have you been all right?"

"Yes. Fine," she said.

Jack looked at her intently. "You're sure, Ruth? I haven't seen you around for the past few weeks. Maybe I'm not supposed to notice, but you look a little tired." He cleared his throat. "I think you'd better tell me about your morning."

She related in an absurdly matter-of-fact manner the sequence of events that had brought her to sit in this hard-backed chair, leaving out the parts pertaining to novels and Felice. "Now that I think of it, I guess we shouldn't have moved the man out of the fountain. It just seemed so wrong to see him in there. Did we ruin some evidence or something?"

Jack rubbed his hands over the dark stubble on his chin. "Don't worry about it. I think we can work around it. Did you know the victim?"

"No. Well, I know his name is, was, Crew Donnelly. He is, was, well, I know he worked as a gardener in town. I think he was employed by the gallery. He planted a beautiful display of flowers in front of the library, too."

"Ever talk to him?"

"Only a 'Good morning' now and again. He wasn't what you would consider a warm, fuzzy sort of fellow. I had a suspicion that he blamed my birds for eating the grass seed he planted at the post office. They didn't do it," she hastened to add, "but they do have beady little eyes and a shifty manner about them, I'll admit."

He laughed again. "I don't usually get such entertainment from murder investigations, but this one has definitely 'got color,' as my wife used to say."

The shimmer of sadness stained his face once again. "So you were headed to the beach and just happened across a body. Talk about the wrong place and the wrong time. Alva didn't know the guy, either."

"Wait a minute." She shook her head. "Oh, actually, it's nothing pertinent. Never mind."

"What?" He put down the stained coffee mug he had raised to his lips.

"Well, I am sure this is wandering off the beaten path. I did have a short conversation with Crew Donnelly just yesterday, but I forgot all about it. Anyway, I was walking the birds down by the lake, and I took a stroll around the gardens while they bobbed. Mr. Donnelly was pushing a wheelbarrow from the greenhouse out to the back lot where the compost piles are kept. I thought it was odd because he had the most gorgeous shrubby plant in the wheelbarrow. I asked him where he was taking it."

"What did he say?"

"He said it was going to the trash heap. I couldn't

believe it, a lovely plant like that, and I made some comment to that effect. He told me orders were orders. I assumed the orders came from Napoleon Prinn. Weird." Ruth toyed with the yellow circle of M&M's on the desktop.

"Is there anything else?" Jack prodded gently.

"Actually, I sort of. . .took it. The plant. After Crew left. It just seemed like such a shame to let it wither in the trash heap. Is that a felony of some sort? Discarded plant theft?"

He laughed long and loud, his tanned face looking suddenly younger. "I don't think so. Believe me, if that's the only crime you ever commit, I'd say you're doing well. And how is the plant, by the way?"

"Hmm. So-so. Rutherford managed to get hold of a branch on the way home, but I think it will recover." She noted his blank look. "He's one of my crankier gulls."

The phone on the detective's desk rang. "I'm sorry, Ruth. I'll let you go before I get knee deep in a phone conversation. Thank you for coming down, and I hope I see you around soon. Do you need a ride home?" When she declined, his dark eyes twinkled, "Are you sure I can't buy you a bag of candy or something?"

"Surely you don't think I would be tempted by a measly bag of chocolate? Now if you've got a bushel basket of M&M's in that vending machine, that's another story." The boyish smile on his face was so very like her son's that it made her heart twist.

He was still chuckling as the door closed softly behind her.

In the hallway, Ruth sagged against the scarred wall under a sudden onslaught of fatigue. She checked her watch. Ten past twelve.

"Well, Ruth," she sighed, "at least you made it to noon. After a morning like this, things could not possibly get worse."

Within hours she regretted the words.

By the time Ruth had returned home from the police station, she was too tired to do anything but fix herself a frozen dinner and stare mindlessly at the television. Then she sat in a near-scalding tub and tumbled into bed before the sun was fully set. She dreamed about rubbery dead men and women shooting people's ears off.

Now, on a frigid Tuesday morning, she was in the kitchen, enveloped in a cloud of sizzling steam. The heat from the oil stung her face, rousing her from a daze. It still seemed so unreal that the same hands deftly slicing mounds of white onions had quite recently hauled a corpse from the Central Park fountain. She could almost feel the slippery rubber on her fingertips.

She was jittery and irritable and she did not want to be in this kitchen at the crack of dawn, slaving over a hot stove for seven feathery ingrates. Martha and Grover were both the victims of BB guns, and the others boasted battle scars from cats, fishing lines, and lures. Phillip had adopted them all, and they got along as well as a totally selfish group of toddlers with no social skills can be expected to. He built them a small covered area where they could weather out the storms, should there be any. The only insurmountable problem was their despicable behavior with guests. The Budges tried a few backyard barbecues, but the birds flattened anyone who held, might have held, or would likely hold in the future any type of foodstuffs. Phillip swore he saw them conspiring before they tripped Pastor Henny and sent him sprawling while they quickly devoured his shrimp canapés.

It was much easier to care for the persnickety bunch with Phillip around.

It was much easier to live with Phillip around.

It was not fair, she thought, that Phillip and God had deserted her on the same awful day. The notion filled her with guilt. Was her faith really so weak? Like the mustard seed that briefly flourished until it met with scorching sunlight? Was God only in her heart when times were happy?

The doorbell caused her to jump, and she gouged her thumb. Grumbling as loudly as she dared, she put down her knife and headed for the door.

The bell clamored a second time before she opened it to Gregory, a pimpled youth sporting a Smashing Pumpkins T-shirt. She wondered if the "smashing" was a verb or an adjective. The boy looked distinctly startled.

"Hello, miss, er. . .ma'am. . .um. . .madam. I am sorry to interrupt, uh. . ."

"No problem, Gregory. I was just doing some frying. What can I do for you? Can you come in for a minute? I've got something on the stove."

His eyes were firmly fixed on his tired sneakers. "No! Er, no, ma'am. I have—it's a delivery." He hastily shoved a stiff white envelope into her hands and scurried like a frightened beetle down the gravel walk.

"Well, thank you," she yelled to his retreating back. He answered by springing onto a dilapidated bike parked at the curb and pedaling furiously toward town.

It wasn't until after she had closed the door that it came to her. She removed her apron and went upstairs to put on her pants.

On the return trip, somewhere around the seventh step,

her nose caught the smell of melting kitchen. Recovering from a moment of frozen panic, she sprinted down the remainder of the stairs and plunged into the black smoke. Locating the stove more by familiarity than sight, she grabbed a sooty pot holder and turned off the heat, but not before some of the oil caught and a plume of flame leapt at her. Slamming a lid down on the boiling pot of oil, she flung open the door to the outside. The cool air felt delicious on her scalding face as she gulped in lungfuls of mist.

The shrill beeping of the smoke alarm pierced the air. There was a distinct smell of singed hair. With a finger, she explored her remaining eyebrow stubble. In the distance came the wail of a siren.

Seven pairs of fluorescent yellow eyes glowered at her.

"Well, I'm sorry," Ruth said, "but I had a kitchen fire."

The glowering continued unabated.

"You're lucky the whole house didn't go up in smoke."

More baleful looks.

"You'll need to make do with the ones I've finished, and the rest will have to wait." Fourteen bandy gray legs vied for positions on the small step.

She solemnly shouldered the platter of cold onion rings and hung two of the greasy treats on each anxious beak. As the gulls hustled off into the yard to devour their treat, the littlest one looked at her with a cocked head.

"Yes, I am all right, Herbert. Thank you for asking." She watched his wedged bottom disappear into the yard before she sat down on the step to cry.

—

She did not need to check the clock later when she heard

the crash against the front door. Her paper was always delivered at precisely ten o'clock, long after the breaking news was no longer newsworthy. Alva was as ruthlessly reliable as zero-hour labor pains. At eighty-two, he was a fine newspaper boy, and apart from occasionally urinating in the Central Park fountain, he was an asset to the community. An odd visitor to the park would complain now and again, but his indiscretions were easily remedied with an extra squirt of chlorine. That little problem was a good deal easier to fix than the latest unwanted addition to the fountain.

"Thank you, Alva," she shouted from her blackened kitchen.

"You got it, sweet cheeks." The endearment was one he applied to everyone, from the waitress at the Rusty Pump to Finny's mayor. "It was a hoot to watch all them fire engines this morning. See ya later."

She felt the accumulated humiliation of having to explain to the fire department the events that led up to one of her neighbors, Mrs. Hodges, calling 911. She didn't think the black smoke billowing from the kitchen was all that momentous, but apparently even small kitchen fires required a code-three response. Within moments her house was filled with the eager, helmeted volunteers of the Finny Fire Department.

Even more embarrassing was the arrival of Monk, who had jogged from his catering business as soon as he heard the news. His face was lined with concern. She was not sure why she felt so jittery when he was around, but the last thing she wanted was to have him witness her kitchen disaster. He was sent away with a hug and a thank you.

Securely zipped in the white Tyvek suit borrowed

from the fire department and armed with Pine Sol and a soft brush, she began scouring her kitchen from ceiling to tile. The blackened grease did not give up without a fight, and Ruth finally tumbled into a chair on her patio, too tired even to remove her green rubber boots. How in the world could she forget about a pot of boiling oil on the stove? Probably the same way she forgot about the pants.

Her husband would have said something comforting about it happening to everyone and quietly helped her clean up the mess, knowing she was thoroughly punishing herself. Then again, he consorted with a whole collection of wild folks whom she didn't even know about. Now that was ridiculous. It was a book, a story, not an affair. Then why did it feel like such a betrayal to find out her life partner, her soul mate, had a secret passion? Even if it was for something imaginary. And now there was no way to know, no way to find out. She was alone with her grief and her questions.

Alone.

The word bounced around in her head. Where was God in all this? Where was the Father who had given her a soul mate and then taken him away, leaving behind only memories and a big fat secret? For what seemed like the millionth time, she wondered why she could not feel His presence anymore. She tried to shove down the anger, but it would not go quietly. "Why did You leave me, too?" she called to the ceiling. Her heart felt as empty as her house.

When she finally made it upstairs again, Ruth reached for her bedside lamp and found the crisp envelope that the boy had delivered before the fire, nestled innocently next to an antique hairbrush. "You'd better be something good, you lousy piece of pulp. I'll never get the grease out of that chandelier." She tore open the stiff envelope and read the invitation inside.

The residential portion of Finny proper tended to huddle along the nostril area of Finny's Nose, pockets of small dwellings clustered along narrow streets radiating outward from the center of town. The farthest-reaching clusters looked down from their precarious perch on the steep cliffs to the ocean. Ruth counted herself lucky to be farther inland when the heavy storm season hit.

As she marched upslope that afternoon, occasionally stepping over one of her bird companions, the houses gave way to fields of ornamental flowers: neat squares of geometrically precise plantings and irrigation systems, cut in between with chocolate brown soil. The palette of colors changed with the seasons, from pastel lilies and snapdragons in the warm weather to vibrant poinsettia reds in the winter.

The nurseries gradually morphed into grazing land and mom-and-pop farms, producing everything from brussels sprouts to bottles of translucent amber honey with the comb floating, fetus-like, inside. Finally, at the top of Finny's protuberance was a grassy plateau, home to the Finny Art Gallery and its outlying greenhouse. At certain opportune moments, visitors could stand on the gallery steps and enjoy a snootful of perfumey chrysanthemums, liquefied cow manure, and the pico de gallo wafting up from the town square.

When Ruth finally led the squabbling parade of birds along the gravelly path in front of the gallery at the apex of Finny's Nose, she paused to catch her breath, noting that the restorations were limping along at the proverbial snail's pace.

That must really frost Prinn's cookies, she thought with a smile.

What was it about that man that made people enjoy goading him? Perhaps it was the arrogance that coated him like a Teflon glaze. He was handsome, successful, educated, certainly. And charming. Flattery was his specialty. Absently she turned and separated two of the gulls. "No, Zachary. Let him alone."

"That is absolutely fascinating."

Ruth peered around at a young lady struggling to haul a box from an old Volkswagen van.

"Pardon?"

"Those gulls just follow you around like, like, ducklings." The redheaded woman ogled over the top of the heavy cardboard box clutched against her stomach.

"Actually, only four of them are gulls. The other three are terns. They are the walking wounded, I'm afraid. None of them could fly away if they wanted to. So they've taken me on as their adopted squadron leader. If they don't get their walk, my shrubs suffer the consequences."

"Do you walk them for their exercise or yours?"

"Both, actually. I came to talk to Mr. Prinn about the gallery dedication, and I thought I'd kill two birds with one stone, so to speak."

"He's not in today. I just talked to his secretary and he won't be back until late this afternoon."

"That figures. I just walked three miles for nothing. Oh well. That's the way things have been going lately."

The woman jerked her head quickly to toss the rusty curls from her face. She let the carton slide down her legs to the ground and brushed her hands on her patched overalls to extend a palm to Ruth. "Red Finchley."

"Ruth Budge. Are you helping with the gallery restoration?"

Red squatted next to the milling birds. "What?" she said. "Oh no. I work for the Shaum Gallery in New York. Mr. Prinn purchased a few of our pieces and I'm delivering them. Good service, eh?"

"Excellent, I'd say. What type of pieces did he purchase?"

"I'm afraid I'm not at liberty to say. All that hoity-toity art secrecy stuff. I guess he wants to keep it a surprise. Do they have names? The birds, I mean?"

"Oh yes. That's Zachary, Rutherford, Grover, Teddy, Ulysses, Herbert, and Martha's the one underneath your van."

"You're kidding."

"No. My husband named them. He thought they had a presidential air. He was a veterinarian, sort of the Pied Piper of maimed birds. We had a real trend going there until Martha was given to us. She had to settle for the first lady."

"And they just follow you around?" Her freckled lips quivered in amusement.

"Well, they sort of live with me. I have a cottage. They probably just stick around for the onion rings. That and the fact that a flightless bird wouldn't last long here."

"They get to have onion rings?"

"I'm afraid that's a naughty treat I indulge them with occasionally. I'm sure their cholesterol levels can handle a little fried food."

The woman stretched out her hand to the nearest bird that inclined his head for a gentle scratch. Ruth thought she had never seen such interesting hands. Red's knuckles were knobby, nicked, and stained like the old leather coin purse Ruth's grandfather used to carry. The nails were bitten down to the quick, and a tide of freckles washed over her hands and crept upward into the dirty sleeves. Staring at them made the freckles seem to dance.

"Which one is this?"

"Ulysses. You can tell by the scar under his eye. He got tangled up in fishing net." During the explanations, three other birds sauntered over and insinuated themselves under Red's outstretched arms, poking pointy beaks into her pockets.

"Oh my." She laughed. "I think I'm surrounded."

"Yes, they are rather forward, I'm afraid, and nosy, too." Ruth pushed a pointy beak out of the cardboard box. "That's none of your business, Grover."

"That's okay. All the really good sculpture winds up sitting in a park buried under gull poop anyway."

"How did Mr. Prinn come across your gallery? I didn't know he traveled to New York."

"It's a very long, boring story, I'm afraid. I really should get this piece of rock into the museum while the getting's good. Maybe I'll see you around."

"Are you staying for a while?"

"I'll be here until the grand dedication or whatever it's called. I'm representing the gallery."

"I just received an invitation for it. You wouldn't believe the inconvenience that envelope turned out to be. Anyway, I'm sure I'll see you there."

"Great. Take care of your feathered friends, Mrs. Budge." She grunted as she heaved the box up onto a dolly and wheeled it toward the museum doors. The gulls echoed with colorful language of their own.

5

The big man at her feet began to make encouragingly conscious noises. With what sounded suspiciously like an expletive, he planted calloused hands on the ground and hauled himself to his knees, drops of blood staining the gravel black.

"Oh. Hey there. I don't think you are supposed to stand up after a head trauma, are you? Officer?" Benjamina reached out a tentative hand.

He ignored her, using the car door handle to pull himself gradually to his feet. He was forty-something, she guessed, creased and weathered from the sun. He had blue eyes that she abruptly noticed were becoming unfocused and beginning to roll back in his head.

"You really need to sit. . ." The breath was squeezed out of her as he collapsed, knocking her down and pinning her shoulders to the ground with his torso. "Oh brother!" she gasped, trying to shove his head off of her shoulder. "I am so not in the mood for this!" As she struggled to free herself from underneath the deadweight, sirens began screaming up the country road.

⌐

Ruth slapped the notebook closed on the scarred library table and felt the tension gradually diminish. Her breath sounded loud in the early evening quiet of the library. It was beginning to be a familiar routine; apprehension as she found ways to put off reading the bits of manuscript, then the anxiety mounting with each page, and finally a depression settling down on her like a mist.

She took a deep breath, trying to match coherent thoughts to her feelings. It was a story, fiction. A fantasy made up to entertain the reader. Wasn't it? But how come Phillip had not told her anything about it? She had assumed the hours of typing would result in a charming collection of memories from a country vet, not a—a what? A mystery? Love story?

Ruth flashed back to the beginning of their own love story. It was a very tiny ad in the *Kansas City Gazette* newspaper that drew her to California; the chance to teach a semester of English at a picturesque high school on the coast. It couldn't have sounded more attractive to a bored woman fresh out of teaching college, desperately looking for a chance to escape the terrible sameness of life on a Midwestern farm.

So it was off to sunny California, where she promptly invested in sweatshirts and long underwear to fend off the foggy chill. Ruth was enchanted by the ever-changing quality of life on the coast; from fog to blazing sunshine, rich soil blending into rocky beaches, and most of all, the sea that seemed to perform majestic foaming undulations for her benefit alone.

Every afternoon when the school bell rang, she hopped into her grumbly Toyota and made a beeline for the beach with a bologna sandwich, a good book, and the warmest coat she could find. It was a wonderful, surreal routine until the day her empty Coke bottle bounced off of the passenger seat and wedged itself under the brake pedal, causing her to crash directly into the rear of a Ducky Diaper Service truck. The impact forced the truck up onto a curb, just enough that its contents disgorged themselves on the top of Ruth's car, burying the front end in pungent baby by-products.

Then Phillip came. He spoke calmly to her and the truck driver before clambering through the goo to release her from her smelly incarceration. She emerged, hands shaking, bleeding from a slight cut over her eye and totally smitten with her handsome rescuer.

They spent a lifetime together, and he had never changed. He loved her in the gentle, steady way that only a soul mate can love. Ruth felt she knew him better than she knew herself. She was totally certain that he would never betray her, certainly not with another woman.

She shifted uneasily in the hard wooden chair. Was that the real root of her unease? The fact that the protagonist of his book was a beautiful woman? A fictional woman, yes, but a woman nonetheless. Her own plainness hadn't ever bothered her before, even on the rare occasions when she noticed Phillip glancing at a pretty woman with admiration. But what about this woman, this lovely, brave woman on whom he had spent so much thought and attention? Maybe beauty was more important to her husband than she had realized.

Or was it that she'd really had no idea what was in his head? After twenty-five years of marriage. No idea at all.

Angrily she piled the library books she had collected into a stack. How come she had not noticed this before? Forty-seven years of life and she had never noticed that something was missing. She wanted to run, run until she reached the ocean, and continue until it swallowed her up.

"I am *so* not in the mood for this garbage."

"What garbage?" The scratchy voice made her jump. Looking up, Ruth saw an old woman in a wheelchair staring at her. Bun Zimmerman. Bun's daughter Wanda was a quasi celebrity in Finny, an extremely talented artist.

"Hello, Bun. I was just, er, reading something." She covered her husband's notebook with her sweater.

The older woman directed her wheelchair closer to the table strewn with books about the care and feeding of fuchsias. "Fuchsias?" Bun's mouth drooped on one side, and her hand lay motionless in her lap.

It was occasionally difficult to understand her since the stroke. "Confucius? Oh. Yes. Fuchsias. I've become interested in them lately. Do you know anything about them?"

"Knew someone who was involved with a plant freak. Even named her child after one. Ridiculous." Bun used her good hand to flip open the heavy textbook and scan a few of the pages.

Ruth laughed. "Did you meet her when you were a nurse?"

"Still am a nurse. You don't stop being who you are because your body gives up on you."

"Of course. I'm sorry."

Bun ignored the interruption. "Too many people trying to be things they're not. Gets them into trouble."

Ruth took note of the small pile of books in Bun's lap. A biography of Eva Perón and two Westerns. Idly she wondered if you could decipher a person's life by seeing a complete list of all the books they had checked out.

Wanda, Bun's daughter, was at the front door of the library. "Gotta go. Taxi's here," she said.

Ruth watched the motorized wheelchair cruise to the front door. Wanda waited until the chair had reached the threshold before she turned and held the door open for her mother.

Ellen Foots, the librarian, was the next person to

materialize at Ruth's table. Ellen was the complete antithesis of the stereotypical librarian. For one thing, she was enormous, a good six-foot-four in stocking feet with the shoulders of a linebacker and the voice to match. Her black hair stood out from her head in tumbleweed fashion, and her face was angular and serious. Rumor held she had started a career as a dental hygienist, but the sight of her bearing down on patients with a hook in hand discouraged too many people from seeking their regularly scheduled dental visits.

"Hello, Ruth. Haven't seen you here in a while." She tucked her chin and looked down as if she were wearing bifocals.

Ruth felt a twinge of nervousness, reminiscent of being sent to the corner in third grade. "Oh yes, Ellen. I've been really busy lately."

"You're never to busy to read, I hope." She arched a thick eyebrow. "That's funny."

"What's funny?"

"The book you're reading here." She stabbed a finger at the fat green volume.

"What about it?"

"Do you know who was the last person to check it out?"

"No."

"The late Mr. Crew Donnelly. Odd, don't you think?"

Ruth thought maybe *creepy* was a better word for it.

"Hmm. Anyway, how about making treats for the rec center show Thursday? Two dozen. No nuts."

As the librarian clopped away in her ankle boots, Ruth looked down at the open book in front of her. "*Most fuchsias will die from overwatering.*"

She had a fleeting thought of Crew Donnelly in the fountain. *Overwatered people don't seem to do well with it, either.* Shuddering, she packed up her books and left.

Ruth often thought Wanda looked less like an artist than an upscale den mother. The pale blue silk tunic and pants cooperatively hugged her ample bust and accentuated her muscular legs. She was an almost handsome woman with a proud, pointed nose and a chin just a shade too wide, and she was constantly in motion, zinging from item to item like an enraged bee punishing itself against the blossoms.

After parking the shrunken bundle in the wheelchair inside the front door of the grocery store, Wanda swooped in, her black ponytail bobbing in her wake. She scooped apples carelessly into a wooden produce basket and careened on to the dairy case.

Ruth watched from behind a pile of onions. People-watching was one of her guilty pleasures. She found people far more entertaining than television. Besides, Wednesdays were buy-one-get-one-free on onions. How could she pass up a deal like that with her gaggle of onion ring fanatics?

Bert Penny, the young clerk who followed along behind Wanda, steadied wobbling towers of cereal boxes and perky displays of toothpaste. He stopped to say hello to the woman in the wheelchair.

"Goood morning, Ms. Zimmerman. How are you today?" he asked loudly. The woman with the puff of white hair regarded him solemnly and nodded.

"You just let me know if you want anything," he shouted before resuming his pursuit of the other Zimmerman.

"Simmer down, Bert," said Luis, the owner of Puzan's Grocery. "Mrs. Zimmerman had a stroke—that doesn't mean she's deaf. Enough bellowing already."

"Oh, right. Sorry, Mr. Puzan."

Wanda called from the cheeses. "Bert, can you please get that wedge of Camembert? I would just about have to crawl over a mountain of cheese to grab it."

"Yes, ma'am." He gingerly reached his way to the pungent wedges at the cheese summit, balancing one foot on the metal rim of the counter and the other on a wooden crate of figs.

"Wait," Wanda said, patting him on the calf, "I think I would prefer Brie instead."

Unfortunately, her request was lost in an avalanche of cheddar, garlic feta, and a tangle of gangly adolescent limbs. Several nearby shoppers came running to aid the stricken clerk. Ruth put down her onions and grabbed the balls of mozzarella as they rolled by.

"Oh my," Wanda sighed, catching Ruth's eye. "I knew that was an accident waiting to happen. I was just telling him that is no proper way to display cheese." She reached out a toe to halt a fleeing wheel of baby Swiss.

A pair of broad shoulders appeared over the conglomeration, and two hands strong grabbed the boy's white apron, hauling him out of the rubble. "Are you all right, Bert?"

Ruth did not know why, but the sight of Monk made her want to duck behind the onions. The caterer set Bert upright.

Bert did a quick inventory of all the important parts and declared himself fit.

"Well, better get a box, son," Monk said, "and I'll help you separate the unfit for human consumption variety from the rest."

Bert trotted away, a fig firmly glued to the seat of his pants. Monk turned his attention to Wanda with barely noticeable regret. "And I suppose you are all right, Ms. Zimmerman?"

"Yes, Monk, and please call me Wanda. It was a shock, though."

He cleared his throat. "Well, er, most cheese accidents are," he said lamely, retrieving his own basket of fresh herbs and root vegetables. "I saw your mother on the way in. How is she these days?"

"Mother? Oh, you know. The same. The doctor says we can't really expect much improvement. It's been years since the stroke. I think it's only downhill from here. Have you given any thought to my offer? I think one of my seascapes would be just perfect in your shop. I would be thrilled to give you one, for a very reasonable price, of course." She tapped a porcelain nail against her front teeth.

Ruth knew Zimmerman paintings were well done, more than well done. Visitors from up and down the coast purchased her bold oils of thundering oceans and wave-battered coastlines. They sold for a hefty sum, and Napoleon Prinn's gallery often devoted an entire section of wall to her work. For a reason she could not articulate, she hoped Monk would decline the offer.

"Well, Ms. Zimmerman, the thing is, I'm an ex–navy man. From my window I can see the old gal, er, the ocean I mean, up close and personal. Having a painting of her would be like, well, like having a photo of your camera. Kind of redundant, you understand."

It sounded as if Wanda was suffering from some type of intestinal blockage until shrill peals of laughter exploded from the artist's mouth, or perhaps her nose.

"You are hilarious. But I am serious; you really should consider it. Several of my larger pieces will be on display for Mr. Prinn's gallery opening. Will you be attending?"

Monk growled his answer. "I'm doing the grub. So what's the new piece the Prinn keeps blathering on about? Is it one of yours?"

Wanda's smile dimmed like a spent bulb. "No. No. I don't know what the big secret is all about. He is very closemouthed."

It was then that Monk caught sight of Ruth hiding in the produce section. "Oh hello, Ruth. How are you?"

Her cheeks burned as she emerged from behind some eggplant. She tried to pull her bangs down over her invisible eyebrows. "Fine, thank you. How are you?"

He ran a hand through his prickly crew cut. "Swell, just swell. I was talking to Wanda." A thought stopped him. "Say, are you going to the art gallery shindig?"

"I think so. I'm not sure."

"Well, I guess I'll see you there. If you decide to go and all."

At that moment the bell on the door chimed, announcing the arrival of a shopper who needed no clanging bells to draw attention to herself. The stunning dark-haired woman picked up a shopping basket and glided into the store, carrying the gazes of all the males in the vicinity with her.

Bert emerged from the back with eyes glued to the voluptuous figure enhanced by jeans and a V-neck sweater. Mr. Puzan hastened to the woman's side. "Hello, miss. What can I help you find?"

"I was just looking for a good Teleme and a baguette. Some Perrier would be wonderful, too." She smiled at him with full wattage and gently pushed a wave of dark hair away from her eyes.

Bert's mouth fell open with an audible *plop*.

Wanda took in the woman's attributes with the subtly hostile look that an almost attractive woman reserves for a drop-dead gorgeous one. Nevertheless, she approached.

"Hello there. I'm Wanda Zimmerman. I noticed you at the gallery yesterday when I was seeing to the details of my pieces on display there. Are you visiting from out of town?"

"Yes. I have business here with Mr. Prinn. Is he a friend of yours?"

"Oh, we've been business partners for years. I am an artist, watercolors and oils. I'm sure you saw some of my pieces when you visited the gallery; they've been on display continually since the gallery opened." She raised an eyebrow before adding, "Are you an artist?"

The woman laughed. "Not exactly."

Ruth was intrigued.

Bert hastened up with a paper bag. "Here's your order, miss. Would you like service out?"

She laughed again. "Well, how about I pay for these things first and then you can carry it for me, okay?"

He escorted her to the cash register and trotted behind her to the door.

Monk nodded cordially as she went by. "Who do you suppose that was?" he said to Ruth. He winked and added in a louder voice, "Maybe she's the new *über*artist he's unveiling next week. Could be he's discovered a new talent. The next Degas, right here in Finny."

"What?" Wanda hurried over. "Did he say the artist is a woman?"

"Not that I've heard; mere speculation on my part."

He smiled sweetly. "I guess we will all find out soon enough."

Wanda smoothed her hair and picked up her basket before she grabbed hold of her mother's wheelchair. "Well, I won't be holding my breath about seeing the work of a prodigy or anything, but at least I know the catering will be exquisite." Wanda pursed her lips thoughtfully. "When can I drop by and sample your wares?"

Monk looked as though he would very much like to give a superbly inappropriate answer. Instead he said good-bye to Ruth and Bun, turned on his heel, and went off in search of the sticky clerk.

7

Ruth deposited the onions safely in the fridge and ate a quick lunch. Then she found herself walking up the graveled walkway to Finny Art Gallery. Sitting on the top step was a giant flowering plant wearing Birkenstocks. The shoes wiggled a bit as Ruth approached, and a round face pushed itself through a gap in the foliage.

"Hello, Dimple. I almost didn't see you there under the flora."

Dimple was Buster Dent's twenty-six-year-old daughter. Buster had raised her single-handedly since her early years when Mrs. Dent ran away with a vacationing investment banker. Buster was wealthy after selling parcels of the land he used to raise pumpkins and Christmas trees to a developer who then raised a crop of tract houses. Buster was a solitary man, with a face full of deep furrows caused by the sun or, Ruth thought, by the harsh glare of life.

Dimple was. . .different. Ruth found that talking to her was like trying to return corn syrup to the bottle; a lot of hard work for very little payoff.

"Greetings, Ruth. Isn't this a lovely specimen?"

"Sure is. What is it, anyway?"

"An upright fuchsia. Single blossoms. The common name is 'Mary Jane.' This particular variety can have red or blue blooms, but as you can see, this little sweetheart is showing off her blues."

"Er, yes." Ruth floundered for a second. "Um, I didn't know you were such a plant expert."

"Hmmm." Dimple gazed at the huge plant in her lap. She was so petite that the pot covered her entire lap.

The silence stretched into the awkward zone.

"How did you come by it?"

"Napoleon didn't want it. I was coming along the path and he carried it out to the landing. He didn't seem to like it at all. Maybe his thumbs are more black than green." She dropped her voice to a whisper. "I suspect all of the fuchsias in his greenhouse are actually fake."

Ruth was just picking up her jaw when she noticed the hint of a smile on the girl's lips and in her huge green eyes.

Whew. Humor.

"Well, that's a lovely bush. Did he grow it himself? It looks like a gorgeous plant to me," Ruth said.

Indeed, the tiny blue flowers seemed to be exploding from every branch. It was like looking at a bushful of infinitesimal bluebirds.

"It was delivered by an unknown giver. I don't know why he doesn't like it. He can be temperamental, you know." She rubbed her tiny gumball nose. "A changing temper mirrors the sadness within."

Ruth tried hard not to let her eyeballs roll back in her head. "Uh, I suppose." Why did she frequently find herself trapped in conversations with this writer of fortune cookie wisdom? How much could that pay, anyway? Did she get paid by the cookie? Good thing she had a rich father.

"How is your fortune cookie business these days?" She knew Dimple exported her fortune cookies to various Asian restaurants along the coast. The cookies were unique; multicolored and intricately twisted, much like the woman who made them.

"Very nice."

Ruth tried to inject some humor into the dying

conversation. "Uh-huh. I guess there's plenty of good fortune in your line of work."

The girl blinked behind the leafy screen.

"Will you be coming to the gallery dedication?" Ruth asked desperately.

"Could be." Dimple struggled to her feet with the giant bush. "I must be off. May the road rise up to meet you."

"Right. You, too, Dimple." She watched the small woman haul the plant down the drive, her blond hair mingling with the branches.

Inside the open double doors, the gallery was undergoing a painful face-lift. The place was a buzzing hive of speckled drop cloths, paint buckets, and overalls-clad men. It smelled of new paint and sawdust. Ruth caught a glimpse of a slender dark-haired woman who vanished down the hallway with Prinn's secretary.

Napoleon stalked back and forth.

"These carpets must be protected," he articulated to no one in particular. "They will be every bit as immaculate when you are finished as on the day they were installed. Is that perfectly clear?"

The nearest set of overalls mumbled something incoherent. The curator continued his reign of terror with serrated comments to the plasterer, the carpenter, and the two Peruvian electricians.

As he stopped to refill his lungs, his harried assistant returned and waved to Ruth before she leaped into the void. "Excuse me, Mr. Prinn, but Mrs. Budge is here to see you and I just showed Ms. Sawyer to your office. I believe she is on a tight schedule today."

Napoleon stepped off the dais and strode toward Ruth with purposeful steps. His lips formed a half smile, and he extended a hand to her.

"I'm surprised to see you here, Mrs. Budge."

Actually, no one was more surprised than Ruth that she was here. She could only chalk it up to an unaccustomed feeling in her gut; a burning speck of curiosity had penetrated the ever-present sadness. She didn't want to analyze it too much in case it went away.

"I'm sorry for dropping by, Mr. Prinn. I don't want to throw a wrench in your schedule. I should have called before coming."

"I am so happy to see you, Mrs. Budge. Let's drop the formalities. Please call me Napoleon, and I'll call you Ruth, if I may. I have been meaning to call you, but as you can see, things are hectic here."

He turned to his secretary, his smile disappearing. "March, tell Ms. Sawyer that I will be tied up for another half hour or so. If she doesn't care to wait, she can make an appointment for another day when I have some free time."

March Browning's eyes widened in exasperation. "I'm finished showing her around the gallery. She has already been waiting for twenty minutes, Mr. Prinn."

"Then she obviously doesn't have anywhere else to be." There was a hint of impatience in his voice.

Ruth contemplated the curator's handsome, angular face, amazed that he could change moods so artfully. His slightly graying hair was obediently settled on his head, the forehead smooth above pale green eyes.

Napoleon must have been a hard name to grow up with, she thought. It just sort of screamed, *Beat me up, I'm different!* He was in his element at the gallery, though. Smooth, elegant, cultured.

"I see this is still very much a work in progress. Will

it be ready in time?"

"It will be in peak shape by Friday if I have to complete the work with my own two hands."

One of the Peruvians eyed the manicured hands with skepticism.

"I'm sure. What is the 'new addition' you mentioned in the invitation?"

"If I told you that, it wouldn't be much of a surprise."

Napoleon rested a hand on her shoulder. His eyes sparkled, and he smelled faintly of cologne. Ruth was annoyed to feel her pulse quicken at the attention. The only man she had shared any physical contact with for the past year was her dentist, and he was protected by sturdy latex gloves.

"And you'd like me to photograph the evening for you?" she asked. She often did freelance work for newspapers and local magazines.

"Absolutely. Obviously, you will attend as a guest for the dinner, and then perhaps we can hire you to take a few shots of the new addition."

"Does it drool and spit up?"

Prinn frowned. "I'm afraid I don't. . ."

"Never mind. Just a small joke."

"Ahh. Well. Anyway, it would be a great service to the gallery if you would photograph the event for us. I know the paper will have some representative there, but I would like to hire someone to document the entire evening."

She contemplated the offer. Why not? She could use the money for the birds' next veterinary visit. Finny had finally replaced Phillip with a new doctor who came with loads of high-tech equipment and fees to match. "Yes, of course I'll do it. But, Mr. Prinn"—she noted his waggling eyebrows and started again—"Napoleon, it really would help to know the nature of the new addition so I'll be sure to select the correct film and filters."

"Sorry. You'll just have to come next Friday. Oh, actually there is one other favor. I'm working on a brochure to advertise the gallery, and I think it would be a wonderful touch to include the greenhouse. It will be in perfect form in a few days. Would you possibly be able to take a few shots? We would be happy to pay you for that, too, of course."

"You don't mind if I just take a peek in the greenhouse now, do you?" she asked.

"Of course not. Just be careful to close the door behind you. I don't want the babies to catch a cold."

She found the remark vaguely disgusting, though she wasn't sure exactly why. "Thank you. I will see you officially on Friday."

Still smiling, he opened the door for her. "I look forward to it. It will be a night to remember."

8

After walking up the low hill, Ruth yanked open the door of the greenhouse, scuttling inside before a chill could settle on the leafy infants. The air closed around her in a slippery blanket.

It took several minutes for her eyes to adjust to the brilliant colors that seemed to explode from each plant. Fuchsias crowded every conceivable inch of counter space and dangled crazily from hanging baskets overhead. The blossoms were tissuey, resembling the fragile paper lanterns that festooned the shop windows at Chinese New Year.

The lower shelves were crowded with similar pots stabbing pointy smooth leaves at the ceiling, topped with frothy crepe flowers that she recognized as some sort of iris. Each container was affixed with a tiny plaque: BLAZING SUNRISE. LILAC STITCHERY. The fuchsias were also labeled. "Gartenmeister Bonstedt. Now there's a lovely little moniker. Rolls right off the tongue."

"He shew'd me lilies for my hair, and blushing roses for my brow. He led me through his gardens fair, where all his golden pleasures grow."

She whirled around and yelped into the face of the speaker.

"I'm sorry. I didn't mean to scare you."

He was a young man, she thought at first glance. Long and lean with windblown curls. There was another impression, a sort of less pleasant aftertaste. He looked . . .scuffed. She suddenly realized he was examining her with equal interest, a look of puzzlement playing about his lips.

"Eyebrows," she sighed.

"Beg pardon?"

"Eyebrows. That's what's missing. I had a kitchen fire; they've been reduced to stubble."

He laughed. "I couldn't quite put my finger on it. Eyebrows. Of course." He chuckled some more then wiped his eyes and gestured to the gently bobbing blossoms. His fingers were long and slender.

"Well? What do you think?" He gestured vaguely. "Do you think Phoebus would approve of this garish display?"

"Umm"—she hesitated—"garish wouldn't be my first choice. It's lovely, I think. Just the thing for a poet."

"But Phoebus was not easily fooled. He could see straight to the root of things, if you'll excuse the pun. Ever see what these spring from?" He stabbed a finger at the potted irises. "Nasty things, corms or rhizomes. They look like shrunken heads. You should see Boney brooding over the bunch, peeling and chilling them. It's unnatural."

She was uncertain how to take this commentary. "Boney?"

"Could it be that you don't know the great man responsible for this wonder? Napoleon Prinn, horticulturist extraordinaire."

"Oh, well, I've never heard him referred to as Boney. Are you a friend of his?"

"Much better than that. We're brothers, twins even. Randy Prinn. Actually, it's Randolph Prinn, but I think Napoleon is pretentious enough for one family."

She could see the resemblance now. This young man seemed like a blurred photo of his brother, darker, softened around the edges, and slightly fuzzy from wear and tear.

"But enough about my family saga. Correct me if I err, but aren't you Ruth Budge, widow of the late Dr. Phillip Budge?"

He took in her surprise. "I saw your biography on the pamphlet for the Women's Photographic Society. President, aren't you?"

"Vice president, actually. Have you been here long? I haven't seen you at any gallery functions."

"Only just came. I don't really think Boney would like to have me attend too many of his galas. I'm not nearly attractive enough. I'm just here for a brief, unavoidable time. I'll be gone before the bloom is off the rose, so to speak." His voice vibrated with laughter.

"Are you vacationing in Finny?"

"No, ma'am. I'm here on business. I write for a coastal paper and I'm covering the stupendous Finny Art Gallery dedication." He took another quick look around the greenhouse and grinned. "I've got to go. All this humidity is terrible for my hair. It has been a pleasure to make your acquaintance, my dear Mrs. Budge. May your eyebrows flourish once again. I bid you farewell."

He snatched up her hand and kissed it with a delicate smack.

She watched him saunter out of the greenhouse, oblivious to the tender plants, which Ruth fancied were recoiling from the chill of the open door. She gazed after him, struggling to recall the rest of Blake's poem. *"With sweet May dews my wings were wet, and Phoebus fir'd my vocal rage. He caught me in his silken net and shut me in his golden cage."*

Blinking her way back to the gallery, she meandered back out to the front entrance and headed off down the steps. She noticed a woman unlocking an immaculate metallic blue Mercedes convertible, the same woman who was in the gallery earlier waiting for Mr. Prinn and charming Bert at the grocery store. She'd heard March grumble the name Summer Sawyer at the galley.

Summer Sawyer was the kind of woman who seemed to be unaccountable to all Newtonian laws of gravity. The top of her was curvaceously plump, accentuated by a tailored wool jacket. The jacket draped over a wool skirt that covered the top of her impossibly long legs. Ruth doubted she could approach those dimensions even standing on her head.

The woman's black hair was cut into a short, sharp bob, which set off her creamy skin. She tossed it out of her face angrily as she yanked open the driver's side door and slid inside. The car zoomed away with a squeal of tires. The lovely Summer, it seemed, had not been at all charmed by her visit to Napoleon Prinn.

Ruth found Monk up to his elbows in clams the next day. This was not unusual for the only caterer in Finny; everyone knew that Thursday was clam day. His name did not cause any confusion anymore, either. Everyone had long ago ceased to wonder at his apparent lack of a first name, or was it a last?

Ruth met Monk the day he became a fixture in the town when he stepped off the U.S.S. *Providence* and left his navy career at the docks. He was famous for his divine cooking and exquisite cable knit sweaters. He had knitted several lovely specimens for Ruth over the years. He broke off from a delicate bellowing of "Spoon River" when she entered the shop and dropped the ladle with a clatter.

"Good morning, Ruth. It's good to see you. You haven't been in for a while." He wiped his hands on a floury apron and hastened to the front counter.

She put down the cardboard box she was carrying and surveyed the hodgepodge of boiling pots and bowls of half-risen fleshy dough. The hair hanging limply in her face reminded her that she had missed her appointment with Felice. Surreptitiously, she tried to pat it back into submission. "You seem awfully busy. Is business looking up?"

"That it is, Ruth. I think I told you that the little weasel hired me to cater his shindig at the museum. I've been getting a head start on the grub. You said you might go—as a guest or the official photographer?"

"Both, I think. The little w—er, Mr. Prinn asked me to photograph the event and the greenhouse. At least I know the food will be well worth the trip." She breathed deeply, trying to remember when she had eaten last. "That smells wonderful."

"At the risk of being immodest, it is. Fish chowder with potatoes and a hint of tarragon. Let me dish you up a pint. On the house." Searching for a spoon, he continued. "You know, Ruth, I've been by your house a few times to visit, but no one answered the door. You were out walking the birds, I guess."

"Well, they do need lots of exercise." The warm swirl of scents was intoxicating.

He began ladling the pungent creamy soup into a Styrofoam container. "I haven't seen you in church for a few Sundays."

Her eyes dropped to her shoes. Lately the thought of singing praises of gratitude and salvation made her feel queasy. She desperately missed the joy that used to fill her heart at service, but she did not know how to get the feeling back. "I think I've been, uh, fighting off the flu. The headaches come and go."

Monk nodded. "Well, maybe Sunday you'll be up to snuff again. I could come by and pick you up."

"Maybe." She put the box down on the floor. "Did Alva tell you about the excitement?"

"Yes, I understand you both had an interesting experience."

"You can say that again. It still seems so unreal to me. It was Crew Donnelly. Did you know him?"

"Nah. We jawed about our days in the service awhile back when he came in for some coffee, but he wasn't a real talker."

"Did he serve with you?"

"He was an army man," Monk said with a touch of

condescension. The screeching coming from the box at her feet suddenly interrupted them.

"You have another commission for me, I gather?"

"Yes, I do. It is so awfully kind of you to do it for me." She knew if she took enough Dramamine, she could make the drive up the coast by herself, but for some reason she continued to ask Monk to do it for her. Was it just to have the excuse to talk to him? She shook the uncomfortable thought away. As she lifted the red towel from the box, a crooked brown neck periscoped out of the opening.

"He's a tiny one, isn't he? Where'd you get him?"

"I found him on the beach. He had a fishing lure imbedded in one wing. It's healed nicely, though. I'm sure he's ready for his own patch of coast, far away from all my crabby critters."

"All right," he sighed, "hand over the little honker." The bird straightened indignantly. "No lip from you, or you'll be tomorrow's special." The calloused hands cupped the gull's slender neck gently. His fingers overlapped hers for a moment.

She lingered for a split second before she pulled her hands away. He had been a friend for so many years, but lately another feeling began to swirl in her brain when she saw him. It was followed by a surge of guilt. "Thank you so much."

"No problemo, dear lady. Maybe you could pay me back in some of those chocolate chip cookies of yours. I haven't had any in months."

"I haven't felt like baking, I guess. Oh no! I completely forgot. I'm supposed to provide the snacks at the rec center today. Ellen hornswoggled me when I let my guard down."

"That's something you never want to do with our librarian. What's cooking over at the rec center?"

"It's a puppet show for the kids. Ellen booked a traveling puppeteer to do a performance this afternoon." She smacked a hand to her forehead. "How could I have forgotten? I've got to go, Monk. I'm supposed to be there with snacks in hand by two o'clock."

"Well, you'd better go, then," he said reluctantly. "Don't want Big Foot on your case. Come back soon, Ruth. Are you busy this weekend? Maybe we could catch a movie."

"Oh, uh, I'm not sure. I don't have my calendar with me." She turned and scurried to the door.

"What about Saturday?" he yelled to her retreating back.

She was already halfway down the sidewalk.

"Ruth! Wait! The chowder!" he called from the door.

She was too far away to hear.

———

The store-bought cookies could almost pass for homemade after Ruth arranged them on a plate and swathed them in plastic wrap, setting some aside for little Solomon whom she knew would stop by later. She made it to the Finny Recreation Center with five minutes to spare.

The kids were gathered in front of the makeshift stage. She recognized Paul Denny with Louella, the lady who watched him during the day, and Solomon and a few other Finny youngsters. In the back row the Solari twins sat on each side of an unusually tall preschooler.

"Hi, Alva," Ruth called, setting down the refreshments.

"Hey, sweet cheeks." Alva waved a sticky hand. "You

want some candy corns?" He held up a crumpled paper bag.

"No thank you."

He nodded and returned to his conversation with the also sticky Solari boys.

Ellen swooped out from behind the shoulder-high curtain hung to conceal the puppeteer from the audience. Her face seemed unnaturally thin in the alarming explosion of coarse hair.

"There you are." She pushed up the sleeves of her Nike sweatshirt. "I was beginning to wonder. We'll keep the cookies covered until after the show so Alva doesn't get into them."

Alva looked up guiltily and shoved his baseball cap farther down on his head. Ruth couldn't hear his muttered remark, but the twins giggled wildly.

Ellen stood before the group and reminded them in stentorian tones to stay seated and quiet. She dimmed the lights and the show began.

It was a charming version of *The Three Little Pigs*. The backdrop was a simple painted canvas depicting a wooded glade, complete with whimsical forest animals and three storybook cottages. The marionettes seemed to have a life of their own as they danced and cavorted. Ruth had trouble believing they were controlled by strings and found herself sitting at the end of a row of mesmerized children, every bit as enchanted as they were. When the show ended, the children made a beeline for the cookies and juice.

Seeing that the librarian had taken charge of cookie monitoring, Ruth slipped behind the curtain. The man in black was carefully hanging up the marionettes in a large trunk, securing their arms and legs with Velcro straps.

"Excuse me. I just wanted to tell you how much I enjoyed. . ." She broke off as she recognized his face. "Randy Prinn! I had no idea."

He squinted at her in the dim light. "Oh, hello, Mrs. Budge. You didn't know I had a side job, huh?" He laughed. "I don't really advertise this one much, in grown-up circles, anyway. Did you enjoy the show?"

"I enjoyed it tremendously. It was amazing. I can't believe you can get those puppets to move like that."

He looked pleased. "It's all in the controller. That's this crosspiece at the top where the strings connect. I've used rod puppets, too, but marionettes really come alive if you know what you're doing." The sarcastic demeanor was gone; he was beaming with boyish enthusiasm. "Do you want to see my best gal?"

He carefully drew a shrouded form from the back of the trunk and unwrapped it. It was a beautiful wooden marionette with curly golden hair and delicate features. She wore a shimmering silver dress and tiny glass slippers.

"Cinderella, dressed for the ball," he said proudly. "I made her myself. Most people these days use plaster molds, but she's made from balsa wood. She's got a hybrid controller that allows me to do some neat tricks." With a few graceful movements of his hand, the puppet closed her eyes and pirouetted.

"She's beautiful. Why don't you do shows full time? It seems to be your passion."

He looked down hastily, busying himself with repackaging his star puppet. "Ah well, I guess playing with puppets isn't really much of a profession, is it? I mean, unless you have the money and time to create your own theater or touring company."

"I don't know much about the business end of things,

but you definitely make these marionettes come to life."

Randy chuckled, his mouth a half smile. "Yeah. I was famous on my block. The kids would come from all up and down the street to see our shows."

"Our shows?"

"You probably won't believe this, but Boney was my stage manager. He painted all the backdrops, too. As a matter of fact, the backdrop I used today is one he painted when we were kids. Amazing, isn't it?" He shook his head. "What a difference a lifetime can make."

Ellen poked her head backstage. "The cookies are gone and I'm closing up now."

"Okay by me," he said as he snapped down the lid of his trunk.

Back at home, Ruth sat thinking about Randy. He was gifted, to be sure; able to make magic out of scraps of wood and string. It was hard to believe that once upon a time, he and his self-absorbed brother had made magic together. Napoleon had about as much whimsy as a dishwasher manual. What a difference a lifetime makes, indeed.

She had been so lost in her thoughts that she hadn't even noticed the passing time until it was almost dusk. Now the waning light brought back all the gloomy feelings again. It was not a fear of dark or strange noises that caused her to turn on every light, but rather a need to fill up all the corners of an empty house. She had spent many nights under piles of down comforters trying to understand these feelings. The only thing that had come out of her self-analysis was a dreadful realization that she was passing time, filling up days, months, years.

Maybe the void had always been there. Maybe she'd just been distracted by a marriage to a wonderful man.

All her life she had been taught to look up, trust God, rely on Him. Had she done wrong by loving Phillip so deeply? Was it a sin to build your life around a person? Was God highlighting her transgression by leaving her so very much alone?

"Oh brother." She exhaled with disgust. "I have simply got to stop watching *Dr. Phil*. You're okay, Ruth. Today, you are okay."

Tomorrow was another story.

Napoleon sat in his office. The cool morning air whispered through his slightly open window. Buck Pinkey watched him over his thick glasses as his bald crown shone under the track lighting. Napoleon crossed, uncrossed, and crossed his legs again.

"This is a lovely office you have here. So airy. Clean." Pinkey cradled the cell phone in his hand. "You've done an outstanding job on this gallery, Mr. Prinn. And the gardens are exquisite." He gestured outside to the profusion of dusky pink and white hydrangea blossoms. "I have tried my hand at growing hydrangeas before, but mine don't show the vibrant colors you have here. Why is that?"

"It depends on the acid of your soil, and the sunlight. They appreciate sun, but not blistering heat." Napoleon shifted in his chair behind the desk. "Mr. Pinkey, may I call you Buck? Can I get you some coffee? Water?"

"Water, sure. Call me anything you want, except late for dinner." He laughed at his joke, the tire around his middle jiggling. He took the glass offered him and patted in his pockets, producing a small pillbox. Extracting a pink pill, he swallowed it with a grimace. "Dramamine. I am itching to get in some fishing while I'm here, but the water is rough." He smiled. "Do you ever fish?"

"No. I don't really care for the water."

"You live on the coast and you don't like the ocean?" He laughed. "I love the sea. You know, I caught a Chinook salmon one time; tipped the scales at one hundred three and a half pounds. Can you believe it? The thing almost killed me, but I hung on. Took three of us to lift it into the boat. Have you ever seen a Chinook? Ugly old monsters with black mouths and gums. The males get this enormous hook-like structure on their mouths when they are spawning. It's called a kype." He gazed out the window into the foggy gardens. "Does the sun ever shine here, by the way?"

"It does, but not until afternoon, typically."

Buck leaned back in his chair and folded his manicured fingers together. "I saw that woman here again, the gorgeous one with the short hair." He smiled slightly. "Who is she?"

"Just a business acquaintance."

"What kind of business?"

Napoleon cleared his throat. "I've done some work with her college, and she wants her students' work shown at my gallery. Mr. Pinkey, you are aware that we have had some trouble here. I am sure you have heard about our gardener. It was an unfortunate accident. The schedule was slightly delayed, but I am confident. . ."

Pinkey interrupted. "Do you have it?'

"I. . ."

"Do you have it?"

"No. But I can have more soon."

"Did the gardener have it?"

"I don't know."

"That's all I needed to know. Thank you." He rose. "I'll meander through the gardens before I'm off to hook the big one. Say, you know of anyone who would charter me a boat? Show me the prime spots?"

Napoleon shook his head. "I'm afraid that's not my area of expertise."

Shrugging, Pinkey left, a trail of musk following him out the door.

Ruth finished snapping a picture of the greenhouse. The newly risen sun provided a fantastic rosy backdrop, just as she'd hoped it would. She had deposited the birds at the pond, knowing they would forage happily until she finished her task. Out of the corner of her eye she saw movement in one of the gallery windows. "Wow. They start their day early," she mumbled to herself. "Maybe I'll just pop in and say hello to March."

The gallery was silent, except for the distant tap of a hammer and the mumbled voices of workers. She walked down the corridor just in time to see March enter Napoleon's office. She waited outside, trying not to listen in on the conversation that floated out the door. "Mr. Prinn, is everything all right?" she heard March say.

Through the open door, Ruth could see the curator reach out a hand toward a painting on the wall, fingers extended but not touching the canvas. "March, did you ever wonder about genius?"

"Genius?"

"Yes. Look at my hands. I have the same number of fingers, tendons, sinews, the same brushes, paints, oils, and canvases as any great painter. I could even look at the same subject one of the great masters studied, yet my paintings would be adequate only. How can that be? Where does the genius lie? It certainly doesn't reside with the desire."

"I don't know, Mr. Prinn. Maybe it's somewhere between the eyes and the hands, a deeper perception combined with a natural talent." She thought for a moment. "Matisse said it is the 'condensation of sensation' that makes a picture. Maybe it has more to do with feeling and seeing the subject than painting it."

He turned away from the painting to face her. "Hiring you was one good thing I did for this place." He pressed his fingers into his temples.

"Mr. Prinn, are you all right? Are you ill?"

He did not answer for a long time as he stood gazing out the window. She repeated the question anxiously.

"Thank you for asking. Please close the door behind you." March quietly closed the door and stood in the hallway.

Ruth opened her mouth to announce her presence, but the woman was so preoccupied she did not turn around. Removing a tiny cell phone from her purse, March punched a speed dial code.

"Things are getting weird here," Ruth heard her say. "There's a man from out of town and he's got Napoleon spooked." There was a pause.

Who in the world is she talking to? Ruth wondered.

"How should I know?" March hissed into the phone. "I've never seen him before, but they know each other." Another pause. "He's from New York. Prinn is really upset. He's talking about genius and how much he appreciates me. I think he's gone around the bend. What should I do?"

She tapped a pearly fingernail. "But what if he changes the schedule? I'm just not sure we should go through with it." More tapping. "Right. Fine. I won't worry, but I need to see you now. Come right away."

She clicked off the phone and walked distractedly into her office. Picking up one of the pictures, she wiped it with the hem of her jacket. "Boy, oh boy, Dad. If you could see me now. What have I gotten myself into?"

Ruth decided now was not the time to visit with March. She turned silently and left the building.

our, five, six. All right. Who's missing?" The surface of the pond was stippled by the busy water striders that stayed out of reach of the birds. She again counted the bunch that milled about her legs.

"Zachary, Martha, oh, it's Ulysses again. What on earth did I do to deserve this?" She knew he must have wandered away from the pond, and if she guessed right, he had probably headed straight for the succulent gallery gardens. With a sigh she shouldered her camera bag and retraced her steps.

Forty-five exasperated minutes later, as she stood peering under bushes, she noticed a man walking down the hill away from the Finny Art Gallery. He was in no particular hurry, strolling along examining the foliage bordering the path. When he reached the bottom of the slope, he nodded his head at her. It was the man who had upset the unflappable Napoleon Prinn and his secretary.

"Good morning. Are you looking for someone?" he asked her. He was well dressed, almost dapper even. Dapper was a shade unusual in Finny.

"Actually, I'm looking for a wayward seagull. Have you seen one around?"

"Surprisingly enough, I have. There was a crabby-looking fellow lurking around the offices behind the gallery. I thought he might be a resident of the grounds or something." He smiled, revealing dazzling white teeth.

"Thank you. I'd better find him before the curator catches him nibbling on the landscaping."

"You seem to know your way around. Could you

recommend a place for rent? Near the water. I'd like something small, a bungalow perhaps."

"Are you from out of town, then?"

"Yes, how rude of me. I am Buck Pinkey. I'm just here for the healthy sea air."

If he was here for the air, she was the Queen of Sheba.

"Ruth Budge. There aren't too many rentals here in Finny. You might check farther up the coast. Half Moon Bay is lovely and has more to offer."

"I'd really like to stay in Finny. It's quaint here."

"Right out of a postcard, some would say."

"Yes. I want to do some fishing. Rent a boat, that sort of thing. I'm staying at the Finny Hotel now, but I'd like something more private. I passed a small cottage as I strolled the beach the other day, white trim and a slate walkway. Is it occupied?"

She watched him closely. "I really couldn't say."

He nodded, and she could see the perfectly unmarred dome of his head, shining like a newly laid egg in the emerging sunlight. "I see. Well, thank you for your time, and I do hope you find your errant bird."

He vanished into the distance. "Why in the world," she wondered aloud, "is he so interested in Crew Donnelly's place?"

⸻

Feeling more than a little foolish, she returned to the gallery and skulked around the back entrance. Checking under shrubs and in flower beds, she made a thorough search for the escapee. Nothing.

Abruptly she stopped scouring the ground for feathers when she noticed one of the back doors was slightly ajar. She caught sight of a feathered behind under the umbrella stand. "Aha!" she said. Slowly pushing the door open another few inches, she crept into the room and stopped short.

Sitting on a recliner was Randy Prinn, and on his lap, March Browning. Luckily, they were facing away from Ruth. Randy was whispering something into March's ear, which made her turn pink. Her normally upswept hair was completely undone. Ruth now had a pretty good idea who was on the other end of March's cryptic phone call an hour before.

"What if something goes wrong? What if he finds out?" March said.

"He won't. He thinks I'm a moron, remember?" Randy said, kissing her on the temple.

Ruth was mortified at what she had walked in on. She felt her face burn, and she held her breath until her chest tightened. Scooping up Ulysses in a football hold under one arm, she ran outdoors like a Heisman Trophy winner sprinting toward the goal line.

The road snarled its way through the spiky shrubbery, grudgingly leaving a narrow crust of gravel along the margins. The sunlight felt nice on her shoulders as she walked briskly, oblivious to the crunch of rocks underfoot. She was thinking about recliners. More specifically, what Napoleon would think about the way in which this particular recliner was being utilized by his faithful secretary and estranged brother. What were those two plotting?

She was muddling through these thoughts when a slip of fluttering white just around the bend in front of her caused her to speed up. Her heart sank as she found the person attached to the fluttery white stuff.

"Oh, hello, Dimple. Are you on your way to town, too?"

The white stopped fluttering and subsided into the tiny fair-haired woman nestled in layers of floating fabric. She smelled of roses.

"Ruth. Greetings of the morning to you."

"Er, greetings right back at you. I was just going to town to stock up on batteries for my camera. Are you going, too?"

"Going?" She looked puzzled.

"To town. Are you going to town?" Ruth repeated.

"To town, yes. I am going to pick up some vanilla."

Ruth was relieved to find some common ground. "What are you cooking?"

"Perfume. I make all my own scents from the flowers in my garden."

So much for common ground. "Well, I guess we could walk together." She could feel her doom gathering around her like flies.

"Yes. The road traveled with a friend is always brief."

It must be punishment for a multitude of sins to be meandering with a woman who thinks in fortunes and brews her own perfumes. The silence lapsed into the intolerable zone. "So what do you think of the gallery renovations?" Ruth ventured.

"Very thorough."

"Yes, they are." The conversation faltered again, and Ruth was unsure how to kick-start it.

"I was there this morning to pick up some work. It was very unsettled," Dimple said as she bent to pick up a feather from the ground.

"Do you work for the gallery?"

The slender woman stopped to untangle her silk scarf from a spiky branch while she considered the answer. "Sometimes. Napoleon asked me to hand-letter the placards for the new addition."

Ruth wondered why everyone referred to the thing as if it were a child. She was also surprised that Dimple used Prinn's first name. "Do you do much work for him?"

"Hmm. I don't think it's very much, no."

"Oh. Well, the new addition, what's it called again?" Ruth asked innocently.

"I don't know. I haven't met the new piece yet."

"Met the new piece? You mean you haven't seen it yet."

"A piece of art is like a person. With great feelings and ideas to express. Don't you agree?"

"Sure." Ruth shoved her hands into her pockets, stifling the impulse to throttle the woman with her own scarf. Then the outer edges of her mind became aware of the sound of a roar bearing down upon them.

Ruth had only enough time to grab Dimple by the ends of her scarf and hurl her in a great fluttering ball into the shrubs. She dove down next to her as a car barreled down around the turn, skidding crazily on the loose gravel.

In a moment she raised her head out of the shrubbery. An engine idled several yards away. She had an impression of a figure looking into the rearview mirror before the car roared off again, leaving them in a shower of gravel and dust.

She coughed and sat up, taking inventory of all her vitals. Her head was spinning. It had happened so quickly.

Ruth had only enough time to gather a vague picture of a dark sedan. Green, gray, blue? She wasn't sure. No license number. Nothing. She tried to stand, but her legs shook so badly she sank back to a sitting position.

After a few more minutes of deep breathing and a quick check of her major parts, she extricated herself from the clawing shrubbery. With a start, she remembered her eccentric companion. Her rubbery legs finally did their job and held her up. "Where did she get to?"

She was relieved to see Dimple lying like a Christmas tree topper in a tangle of gauze and bushes.

"Are you all right?" Ruth panted.

The woman gazed at the sky, hands neatly clasped across her abdomen. Ruth wasn't sure if she was still considering the last question or applying her thoughts to this one.

"The road to adventure is uneven and perilous," she said.

Ruth plucked off a juniper berry hanging by a hair above her stubbly right eyebrow, thinking about the weird set of events that had turned her life around lately. "Ain't it the truth."

The sun was just beginning to set as Ruth finally hobbled in her front door. Her feet were aching and there was a definite spasm developing in the small of her back from her dive into the junipers. She concluded that when you start measuring your life in decades instead of years, that dated feeling is inevitable. Especially when you are leaping away from out-of-control vehicles.

She spent the rest of the afternoon soaking in a tub and trying to nap. Though she tried her best to put it out of her mind, the fact surfaced. She and Dimple could very easily have been killed by the crazy driver. Was it someone in a hurry? Just a moment of unfortunate carelessness? Another thought froze in her mind. Or was it someone on a mission to kill?

"Lord, help me," she breathed more out of habit than hope.

Ruth was just finishing her dinner of canned ravioli when the doorbell rang. After a moment of unreasonable panic, she gave herself a shake, assuring herself that the stove was safely asleep for the night. Who could be wanting to see her? She was very accomplished at the commando crawl to stealthily ascertain the identity of visitors without the need to open the door. Many a chicken broccoli casserole and plate of homemade cookies had been left on her doorstep in the months following the funeral.

The bell chimed again.

After a torturous minute of indecision, she yanked open the door.

Detective Denny was standing on the front step, hands jammed into the pockets of his brown trousers. "I'm sorry to call on you so late. I heard about your accident today and I came to check in on you."

"News travels fast. How did you hear about it?"

"Alva. He said he stopped you in town to ask how many licks it would take to get to the center of a Tootsie Roll Pop. He noticed your grubby knees and hair and figured you'd been in some sort of a scrape. How come you didn't report it?"

"I was sort of in a daze, I guess. Please come in." She led the detective into the kitchen and gestured him into a comfortable yellow chair. He gently fingered the fuchsia dangling off of the plant stand where she had plopped it.

"Is this the boasted fuchsia?"

She blushed. "It's called a Heston Blue."

"Doesn't smell?"

"Not a bit. I think it's really so odd that our gardener extraordinaire seems to have such an aversion to these plants. This is the second one I've encountered that Napoleon seems to actively loathe."

"Weird. But then, he kind of marches to a different beat."

"That is definitely true." She shook her head. "I'm sorry. I haven't had visitors in a while. I've forgotten all of my hostessing skills. Let me fix you some coffee and a muffin. I discovered them in my freezer when I decontaminated my kitchen."

"I heard about that. How are the eyebrows?"

"I'm not expecting to see them anytime soon. I think I'll have to fill them in with magic marker from now on."

"Not to worry. I couldn't tell at all."

"You're a sweet liar, Detective." She poured the coffee and served him a succulent muffin.

"Please call me Jack. We've been through enough together to drop the Detective and Mrs. stuff. Don't you think?" After what they had been through, he thought of her as more of a mother than his own flesh and blood.

She nodded. "And how is Mr. Boo-Boo these days?"

"Ecstatic as usual." Jack drifted back to their first meeting. Mr. Boo-Boo was the impetus for their introduction. He was the most unnatural collection of canine parts ever assembled. Tipping the scales at just over ninety pounds, his gangly body was covered with wiry whorls of hair, and his head was a compact bony wedge. The poor beast's only attractive feature was his eyes, one a soft green and the other a startling blue.

It was these amazing peepers that proved irresistible to Lacey Denny when the dog catapulted into the front seat of her car in the Shop and Go parking lot. He licked her face happily, forgave her for not bringing along any doggy toys, and waited patiently to be driven home. No amount of coaxing or threatening could remove that dog from the passenger seat.

Jack had never shared his wife's conviction that the dog was keenly intelligent. He watched Lacey and Paul throw endless weekly editions of the *Finny Times* and hopefully command, "Fetch!" He would never forget his astonishment when, one overcast morning, the dog trotted out to retrieve the paper. It took him forty seconds to maim the edition before trotting victoriously into the kitchen with a slippery rubber band clenched between his teeth. Mr. Boo-Boo fetched fourteen rubber bands before Lacey admitted defeat.

He remembered, too, the desperation he felt when Mr. Boo-Boo escaped two months after Lacey's death. The unlatched gate, the explosive panic. He spent two hours scouring every pungent corner for the dog and winding up completely desperate in front of Ruth's front yard. She was hacking away at some wickedly spiked bougainvillea. She said, "Are you all right, Detective?"

He could not give words to the desperate aching in his gut, the black fear that welled up inside him like a poisonous mist. He could not lose this dog, the only link to his little boy's world. "My dog. . ." was all he could manage to gasp.

She had looked at him for a long minute, reading the despair washing over his face. Jack could still remember the tiny drop of blood on her cheek where a thorn had pricked her. "Yes," she had said simply and put down her clippers. Together they walked out into the copse of trees behind her house and began whistling for the elusive dog.

Mr. Boo-Boo made his appearance shortly thereafter, climbing out from under a tangle of branches. He smelled strongly of mold, and his matted hair carried an impressive sampling of foliage. He bounded over and sent Jack sprawling in a puff of dirt.

His thoughts returned to the present. With a sigh, he put down his coffee.

"Boo-Boo is his usual slobbery self. My current undertaking is to teach him how to greet people without causing any contusions."

Ruth smiled then asked softly, "And Paul?"

"He talks to the dog. That's all. Just the dog. I can't even get him to smile. It's so frustrating. He was so happy before. . ." His voice trailed off.

Lacey, his beloved wife and the mother of their precious boy, had walked out to the mailbox while Paul watched from the window. She collapsed at the end of the driveway, dead of a brain hemorrhage.

Paul, Jack surmised, had called her and called her, but it had been a good hour before a neighbor noticed and dialed 911. By then the boy was crouched into a little ball with his hands around his knees, his face terribly white, huge Mr. Boo-Boo cradling him protectively.

Jack snapped out of his recollections with a shudder. "The psychologist says he needs to feel safe again. He needs to be sure that I'm not going to leave him, too." He shook his head. "How can I promise him that, Ruth? How can I assure him that his mother was gone in a heartbeat but I somehow will be here forever?"

She sighed. "I don't know. I still think I hear Phillip singing in the shower sometimes. I guess I am supposed to have gleaned a deep wisdom about the mysteries of life and death at my age. All I know is, time does not heal some wounds, Jack. There is just not enough of it." She stopped talking as her eyes filled with tears.

He busied himself drinking coffee while she recovered herself. "You know, Ruth, I haven't seen much of you in a year, and here is our second visit in a week. I don't know whether to be glad or alarmed." The detective wrapped his hands around the steaming mug, happy to be back on safer conversational ground. "Do you want to tell me what happened today?"

She related the events in a rough chronological order. "The strange thing is, I got the distinct impression that the car stopped down the road for a minute and then kept going. Was Dimple able to add anything else?"

He gave her a telling stare. "Not unless you count her advice about fate being kind to the penitent or something to that effect."

"How is the Donnelly investigation going?" she asked.

"Slowly. No family that we can locate. His cottage didn't really tell us anything except that he was planning to leave soon."

"I don't suppose he fell headfirst into the fountain and drowned accidentally?"

"Nope. The medical examiner says he drowned after someone clobbered him with a blunt object. He probably fell backwards into the water with or without help sometime between 11:00 p.m. and 4:00 a.m."

"It wasn't a robbery?"

"Doesn't seem to be. He had a wallet on him with a couple of bucks in it. Nothing was disturbed at his place."

Jack massaged his face with one hand then straightened up suddenly. "It's my beeper," he said, consulting the tiny screen. "I've gotta go."

At the door he paused. "Did Crew Donnelly strike you as the type who would appreciate fine art?"

She considered this. "He seemed more like the type who would appreciate a nice carburetor."

"That was my take, too. His cottage was bare bones, no embellishments at all."

She waited. He turned to face her on the darkening doorstep.

"So why do you suppose he had a Zimmerman seascape lying on top of his bed?"

Ruth wasn't really sure what brought her to the door of Prinn's greenhouse on Saturday morning. It seemed that curiosity had infected her like a hostile virus. She had spent the wee hours searching for Phillip's novel and worrying about things, some phantom detail niggling at her, prodding at the corners of her mind. She couldn't understand why Prinn would send away a gorgeous plant, the same plant Donnelly had trucked off to the dump just before he was murdered. The conversation with Jack only made her feel even more strongly that something was fishy in the town of Finny.

The sunlight caught the greenhouse glass, which reflected the light, sending it spinning crazily in all directions, like some great winking insect eye. She couldn't see clearly in the windows because of the opaque covering of moisture.

How odd.

The door to the precious temple of greenery was ajar. She was reaching for the handle when a missile came sailing out and smashed onto the slate stepping stones at her feet.

Rusty shards of terra-cotta pot entwined with the branches of a leggy green plant. The whole mess was dotted with exquisite white flowers edged in pink, identical to the plant she had rescued from the compost pile.

"This is intolerable!" hurled a voice on the same trajectory that the plant had taken a moment before. The curator's voice broke off as he emerged from the greenhouse and caught sight of Ruth as she stepped forward into the settling dust and fragrance.

He brushed his hands together and smoothed his tie. "Ruth. I didn't know anyone was standing there." His laugh was nervous. "Are you hurt?"

"No. You are a pretty strict disciplinarian with your plants. What did this one do? Stay out after curfew?" She bent and plucked a fragile white blossom from the crushed plant.

"Well, I am a perfectionist, I'm afraid. They must be perfect to stay in my greenhouse. I don't tolerate mediocrity." The flush was gradually receding from his cheeks. "I wouldn't want to bore you with the specifics."

"It won't bore me. Actually, I have been reading up on fuchsias lately. What is the name of this variety? I've forgotten."

The flush crept up his throat once again. "I can't recall."

"It's a man's name, isn't it? Henley, Hestor, Heston. Heston Blue. Odd name, don't you think?"

"I'll just get a broom and sweep this up. Please forgive my fit, Ruth."

"I saw your brother's show Thursday."

Napoleon looked blank.

"Randy's puppet show. At the rec center."

He was uncharacteristically silent for a moment. His lip curled in disgust. "I didn't realize he was still playing with puppets."

"Randy said you painted the backdrop when you were younger."

A strange look of confusion washed over his face. "The backdrop?"

"The country scene with the trees and the little thatched cottages."

His mouth fell slightly ajar, and she saw for the first time some genuine emotion seeping through the mask of self-assurance. "That old backdrop? He still uses it?"

"Yes. He said you could make magic on a canvas."

He blinked again and closed his mouth. "Magic. That was years ago, Ruth. I don't have time to stroll down memory lane at the moment. If you'll excuse me, I really need to get this mess cleaned up."

He walked stiffly down the path toward the gallery. As he passed her, a sweet scent whispered along with him.

"Of course." Ruth made sure the greenhouse door closed completely before she turned to go.

He stopped a few yards away. With his back still turned away, he asked over his shoulder, "Was it good?"

"Pardon?"

"The show. Was it good?"

She thought for a minute. "It was magic."

At the corner of Whist and Main, a familiar car was parked at the curb, its shiny finish blinding Ruth momentarily as she rounded the corner. The driver's window was open. A woman sat in the front seat having a furious conversation with herself. No, not herself—she was speaking into a tiny cell phone hidden under a sheaf of hair. It was the woman Ruth had seen driving angrily away from the gallery. The angry bob of the head and the increasing pitch told her it was not a pleasant conversation.

The woman yelled, smashing the cell phone repeatedly into the dash until a piece of the black plastic broke off and sailed through the air, landing just in front of Ruth's shoe. The woman peered out of the window. "I'm sorry. Did that thing hit you?"

"No, I'm fine." Ruth bent to retrieve the piece and walked over to the woman as she unfolded from the car. "Do you want it back?"

"Sure." She exhaled loudly as she dropped the plastic into her slim leather clutch. "I'm sorry. I guess I'm under some stress lately. Don't you have a gym or anything in this town?"

"Only the one at the high school." She felt the need to defend Finny. "Lots of people relax at the beach, running, hiking, boating, what have you."

"I prefer climate control to outdoor breezes. I don't think we've met. I'm Summer Sawyer."

"Ruth Budge. I saw you at the gallery. Are you in town on business?"

"Yes, I am the dean of the art department at Pomponio University. I came to attend the dedication."

"Why?" Ruth asked bluntly.

"Why?"

"I mean, is there a special connection between your college and the gallery?"

Summer fixed her with an intense stare. "Napoleon is the connection. He has donated generously to our art program." She turned and opened the car door. "It was nice meeting you, but I really need to go. I heard there is a salon around here. Am I getting close?"

"Sylvia's. Just keep going this direction; it's two blocks down on the left-hand side. One of the gals is on vacation in Fiji, so you may have to wait."

"Right. Thanks."

Ruth watched her drive away. It would be interesting to see what this elegant woman looked like after enduring a Sylvia hair treatment. Sylvia only knew two styles:

short á la a Marine Corps buzz cut or curly as in the well-groomed poodle look. Chuckling to herself, she continued her walk home, puzzling as she went.

The town of Finny was getting stranger by the minute. A beautiful woman with some anger management issues arrived in town for the gallery dedication, only to be snubbed by the gallery owner. Prinn's behavior was a mystery, too. This self-assured, arrogant man was a painter of whimsical theater magic. What was that emotional response to news of his brother's show? Disgust? Envy?

These confusing thoughts followed her all the way back to her cottage. As she walked into her kitchen, the fuchsia seemed to wave gently at her.

Something from the encounter with Napoleon tried desperately to surface in her brain. She closed her eyes and saw the fuchsia smashing to the floor, saw Napoleon's face tight with anger as he brushed by her.

It came to her like a lightning bolt.

Fuchsias have no scent. Who, then, left the musky scent of roses on Napoleon Prinn's clothing?

It could be only one person.

Dimple Dent.

14

The detective had all but decided he should have stayed in bed. Working on Saturday wasn't the problem—he was used to that. It was the way the whole day started that added to his funk. While getting out of bed he stepped on a sharp Lego and skidded to the floor with a thump. Limping into the bathroom for a Band-Aid, he found a naked Paul unfurling a second roll of toilet paper and dumping it into the potty while Mr. Boo-Boo the dog panted encouragingly. Jack chastised the boy soundly until Paul galloped down the hall and hid under his bed. Jack tried apologizing and cajoling as the dog gave him a profoundly disappointed look, to no avail.

He felt a heavy sense of paternal failure as he drove to work.

Lacey was just better at kid things. She always knew how to talk to Paul without letting minor problems escalate into major productions. And how did she do that kissing thing? Ouchies were supposed to be kissed, but his lips just didn't have the same healing power hers did. Try as he might, he was not cut out to be a mother.

He wasn't sure he was great father material, either.

At the office he caught his first whiff of impending disaster when he encountered all three of his officers gathered mournfully around the deceased coffee machine, empty mugs dangling from their fingers.

Three professionals who can foil bank robberies, find missing children, and subdue armed felons—thrown into complete turmoil by a backfiring Mr. Coffee.

"Please, somebody tell me the coffee machine is not still broken."

"The coffee machine is not still broken," Nathan Katz announced. "The coffee is just a tad weak." He handed Jack a mug of barely warm water.

"Oh man."

"My sentiments exactly," said Nate.

So much for Saturday.

The library should have been the first stop for the detective, but facing Ellen Foots with no coffee in his veins caused him to procrastinate. Pulling up to the Finny Art Gallery instead, he heaved his decaffeinated body out of the car and through the front door. He heard the yelling long before he saw the five furious people in the lobby.

"What is that piece of ugly s'posed to be?" Jack recognized Buster Dent, Dimple's father, poking his calloused finger toward a canvas-covered lump. "You call that thing art?"

A flushed, red-haired woman leaped out of her chair and confronted him. "That happens to be a Carmine, you clod! It's worth more than any Motel 6 art you've got hanging in your house."

Dent ignored her and turned on Napoleon. "I didn't pay for no cryin' lady statue, Prinn. You promised me somethin' pretty. I came to this preview expecting to see a landscape or some sunset somewhere. What is this thing?"

"Mr. Dent." Napoleon Prinn's smooth voice rose over the din. "I assure you the sculpture is a very valuable piece of art. A Carmine sells for well over five times what other marble pieces do."

"I thought you were buying a painting. And what kind of a name is that? Carmine? Don't he even have a first name? Where's he from, anyway? One of them third world countries?"

"It worked for Picasso, da Vinci, El Greco, Van Gogh, Donatello, Michelangelo." Red ticked off the names on her fingers. "Shall I go on? But you probably don't even recognize those masters. . . ."

"He is a very elusive artist. He has never been photographed, nor does he appear at any exhibitions of his work. The entire art community agrees, however, that his work is simply exquisite." Prinn moved toward the sculpture. "If you'll only look. . ."

"He must be elusive," said a black-haired woman Jack had never seen before. She sat gracefully in a chair observing the group, one shapely leg crossed over the other. "I've never heard of him, and neither have any of my colleagues."

Red stepped in front of him. "Don't even bother to educate them, Mr. Prinn. They obviously know as much about sculpture as they do about manners. I think I should take this back to the Shaum. Our curator would be horrified to see it so unappreciated."

"Now, Ms. Finchley, there is no need for. . ." Prinn was momentarily distracted. "What are you writing?"

Randy, standing next to an anxious March, looked up from his notebook and laughed. "The most interesting piece of behind-the-scenes hysteria that I've come across in years. This is really great stuff, Boney. It'll make great copy."

At that moment, several things happened simultaneously. March clasped Randy by the forearm as Napoleon grabbed him by his shirt collar, Red and Buster stepped forward reflexively, and Jack cleared his throat.

Everyone froze in a ridiculous tableau.

"Good morning, folks. Am I interrupting anything?"

After a second of shocked stillness, the gathering smoothed their collective clothing and lowered their voices several octaves. Prinn stepped forward. "Hello, Detective. To what do I owe this unexpected visit?" His mouth was crimped into a less-than-welcoming grimace.

"Just some routine questions about that gardener-in-the-fountain problem. I'm sure you have a few minutes to chat, don't you?"

"Of course, but perhaps we could talk at a later time. We were just having a strategy session before the party on Friday. You know Mr. Dent and March Browning. This is Red Finchley, from the Shaum Gallery in New York, and this"—Prinn turned, gesturing to the statuesque woman in the chair—"is Summer Sawyer, dean of art at Pomponio University."

"Pleased to meet you." Jack took Summer's slender manicured hand for a moment before turning. "And you are?" He extended a hand to the man with the notebook.

Randy jammed the chewed pencil into the curly hair behind his ear. "Randy Prinn. I write for the *Coastal Times*. I cover all the gallery openings, up-and-coming artists, new exhibits. You know, riveting stuff like that. So would you like to give an official quote about the murder?" He leaned forward eagerly.

Napoleon put his hand on Jack's shoulder. "Let's chat in my office, Detective. March, would you join us, please? I will finalize the rest of the details with you all tomorrow." He led the way to a plush room overlooking the blooming gardens. There was a tantalizing aroma of freshly brewed coffee. None was offered to the detective.

"What can I help you with, Detective?"

"It seems you have your hands full with your own problems, Mr. Prinn. Trouble among the ranks?"

"Not at all, not at all. Just a difference of opinion. Nothing a short discussion won't mend."

"The reporter—is he your brother?"

Prinn cleared his throat and clasped his hands firmly on the lacquered top of his desk. "Yes."

"I've never met him before. Does he live around these parts?"

"He doesn't live anywhere. He's a drifter." The words fell like shards of glass. "Shall we move on to your questions, Detective Denny?"

"Sure. Before we do, though, what is a dean from Pomponio University doing here in Finny? Isn't that down near Pescadero?"

"Yes. Ms. Sawyer was working with me on an exhibit of her students' work here in my gallery."

"Was?"

"Well"—Napoleon looked apologetic—"actually, it was a favor for a friend of mine who is on the board of directors there. It is a fine university. I did some undergraduate work there myself, and of course, I have contributed to their efforts to beautify the campus. Have you heard of the Prinn Gardens at the student commons?"

"I'm afraid I haven't."

"No matter. One of the chancellors asked me to feature some of the work from their school of art at my dedication. I agreed, to help promote the university."

And it wouldn't hurt your reputation to be a benefactor to a prestigious college, either, Jack thought.

"To make a long story short, the pieces that Ms. Sawyer brought me were simply abysmal. I couldn't accept such juvenile work at my gallery. I have a reputation to protect, and I had to tell Ms. Sawyer to cancel her participation in the dedication."

More likely, Jack thought, she had voiced an opinion like the one he heard today, questioning Prinn's judgment. "And I imagine she found that uncomfortable to explain to her superiors?"

"I imagine, since she came back today to try to change my mind. I do feel badly for her; she is so intent on being a trustee there someday; this probably set her back a rung or two. I really didn't have a choice, you know. The integrity of my gallery must come first." He looked for affirmation from March, who became suddenly busy looking through her notebook.

"But I'm sure you have more important things on your mind. Shall we take care of your other questions?"

Jack flattened himself into the brocade chair as best he could. "All right. I understand Crew Donnelly was an employee of yours. How long did he work for you?"

"A matter of six months or so. I hired him for maintenance of the grounds, sometimes a delivery or two. That sort of thing."

"What do you know about him?"

"Not much. We didn't chat often."

Jack eyed the immaculate suit and manicured nails. He imagined the curator didn't speak to any of the hired help, except perhaps to the pretty lady seated next to him. "Ms. Browning, isn't it?"

She glanced nervously at Prinn before nodding.

"What do you know about the victim?"

"He did some work around town, at the library and such. When Mr. Prinn asked me to find a gardener, I asked Ellen Foots about him. She said he hadn't been in town long. He was checking out books one afternoon, and he heard her talking about landscaping the breezeway. He offered his services and told her if she didn't like the results, she didn't have to pay him. The results were fabulous, as you can see for yourself, so we hired him after the library project was finished."

"Was his work here satisfactory?"

March glanced again at Prinn. "I believe the grounds were very well maintained."

"He was rather free with advice at times," Prinn interjected. "To be perfectly honest, Detective, I intended to let him go at the end of the summer."

"Did he know that?"

"No. I just decided a few days ago when I caught him in the greenhouse for the second time."

"Gardeners aren't allowed in the greenhouse?"

"Not in my greenhouse. My plants are extremely sensitive, and I will not have people tramping in and out uninvited. I explained this several times to Mr. Donnelly, but he nonetheless intruded on at least two occasions."

"So you decided to fire him?"

"I was intending to let him go, yes."

"Where did he live?" Jack knew exactly where the gardener lived, having been to the place several times since the murder. He wondered how well the curator knew his employees.

"He rented a bungalow on the beach, I think. That small place that the inland people rent in the off-season."

"The inland people" was the local term for everyone living outside of Finny to the eastern seaboard. "I guess I'll take a trip to the beach, then." He struggled loose from the brocade. "I don't suppose you know who wanted Crew Donnelly dead?"

Prinn stiffened and March blanched. "No, Detective, I'm afraid we don't," Prinn said.

"Oh, one more thing. Do you think I could get a peek at your greenhouse? I'll be careful not to trample anything."

"Of course. March will show you around on your way out."

"Thank you. I'll be seeing you soon." The door closed softly behind him.

15

*H*er arm throbbed. *The bulky silver and blue splint the doctor had welded to her two broken middle fingers made her feel as though she were continually committing an obscene gesture. She would have, should have, gone straight home to a pint of Chunky Monkey, but now the cop was asking to see her.*

She pushed open the heavy door, knocking softly as she entered the room. He was lying with his eyes closed. Asleep, she thought. Poor guy. Everywhere she could see seemed to be either scratched or blue, except for his face. That looked drawn and pinched. Maybe he always looked drawn and pinched. She'd only seen him unconscious and passing out. Benjamina cleared her throat delicately.

Nothing.

She coughed slightly.

Not a flinch.

"Hello!"

She intended to murmur a greeting, but it must have come out more forcefully than she meant, because his eyes shot open and he half jerked upright like a jack-in-the-box with lumbar problems.

He blinked several times. "Afternoon, ma'am. Are you looking for someone?"

Why does saying "ma'am" make everyone sound like they come from Mayberry? *"Actually, I was told you asked to see me."*

He looked totally befuddled. Probably the medicine, she surmised.

"Do I know you, ma'am?"

"We've met briefly. You were more or less unconscious at the time."

"Unconscious?"

She heaved an impatient sigh. Medicine aside, there was a pint of Chunky Monkey and a prescription for Vicodin at home with her name on it. "I am the gal that found you on the side of the road."

"Gal?" A moment's hesitation. "Did you help the fella out?"

"What fella?"

"The man who was at the scene. Ben, I think he went by."

The clouds parted. "Oh, I see. You were expecting someone else. I'm afraid you'll have to settle for me. I am Benjamina Pena. Most people call me Ben."

"You? I can't believe. . ." he stammered.

The turmoil of the day finally caught up with her. Annoyance crept in underneath the throbbing. "You can't believe what? That you were rescued, for lack of a better word, by a woman? Is that just a little too much for your macho mystique to handle? Well, there weren't any other manly rescuers around, so I did the best I could."

The man's face became distinctly pink under the fatigue. He passed a hand over his eyes briefly. "They told me there were shots fired, that someone scared off the guys who jumped me. I just. . ."

"You just assumed it was a man. Of course. I can't believe this. Here I am driving along, minding my own business, and there you are in the middle of the road, not even having the decency to remain conscious long enough to radio for help. Do I look like a person who enjoys radioing dispatch and shooting armed thugs? Do I?" Her voice rose.

He lay watching her, mouth agape.

Her tone edged up another few notches. "And you just

had to get up after I TOLD you not to and fall down on me. Do you see these fingers? They were perfectly good this morning. Do you know what I do? I am an art teacher. I PAINT! How do you suppose I am going to do that without my fingers?"

The man cleared his throat. "I sincerely apologize, Ms. Pena. I am very grateful for your help."

Benjamina gathered herself. "Well. All right then. I may have been a little harsh. It has been a very strange day, Mr.—Officer? Is Roper your first or last name, anyway?"

"First. My name is Roper Mackey. Just call me Rope."

"Okay, Rope. Listen, I think I'd better be going. I'm sure you need to rest, and I need carbohydrates."

"Thank you again, Ms. Pena." He extended a dry, calloused hand for her to grasp. "By the way, there is one thing I really need to ask you."

"What's that?"

"What exactly is a troglodyte?"

A smart tap on the door sounded like a gunshot in the perfect silence of the house. Ruth dropped the manuscript in a heap on the floor. In a fit of cowardice she had left a message on Monk's machine when she knew he was at work. Her headache was back, she had said; she would have to miss Sunday service. With a quiver of guilt she knew it was not her head that was sick, but her spirit. Maybe Monk had decided to come check on her on his way to church. For a moment, she stayed in the chair, frozen.

"Hallo? Anybody home?" called a voice attached to the face peering through the wire mesh.

Ruth rubbed sweaty palms on her pants and unlatched the screen. "Well, hello, Red. It's so nice to see you. Come in."

"Thanks. I don't usually barge in on people, but I got bored just walking up and down the beach talking to myself, so I thought I'd just visit the only person I know in this town. A guy named Monk told me where you lived. I hope you don't mind the intrusion." Her voice was low.

"Not at all," Ruth said. It took a supreme effort to summon up charm, to stir up the silence she was steeped in. "I'm happy to have the company of an unfeathered friend. Would you like some tea or ice water? Lemonade?"

"Water would be great."

Ruth bustled off into the kitchen and returned with two yellow glasses. As she returned to her guest, she was dumbfounded to see Red skimming through the pages of her husband's writing.

"I hope you don't mind," said Red, taking the glass. "It was on the floor. Are you a writer?"

"Uh, no. No. My late husband was, I think," she stammered lamely.

"Well, how does it end?"

Ruth stared at her blankly. "What?"

"The story. What happens to the girl who saved the cop? How does it end?"

After an endless pause, she answered. "I don't know. I haven't gotten that far. I'm not sure it was ever finished."

"Wow." She nodded her head thoughtfully for a moment. "Are you going to do it?"

"Do what?"

"You know. Finish it."

Ruth's mouth dropped. She managed a weak "Me?"

"Why not? You've got the beginning, don't you?"

"Well, yes. I guess I do, but I really have no idea how

he was going to end it or, uh, anything like that."

"Hmmm. You didn't discuss it with him?"

"No." Her stomach did a sudden flip-flop. "No, not really."

"Oh." Her brows knitted together like copper-colored springs. "That means you get to make it up on your own. You know, write your own fantasy ending."

"I am not a writer by any stretch of the imagination. I am just an amateur photographer in an itty-bitty town. Speaking of towns, how do you like ours, anyway?" She felt desperate to change the subject.

"It's very quaint, I suppose. In a sleepy fishing village sort of way."

Ruth sipped, watching the amber eyes that watched her. Tendrils of hair floated around Red's face like an unraveling hem. Ruth found herself warming to this vibrant girl. Red's eyes wandered to the rusty hydrangeas outside, spots of color in the gathering mist. "So how can you stand it here every day, with the awful fog?"

"You get used to it, I guess."

"Yeah. How does that poem go? The one about the neighbor holding the lamp until her friend's eyes adjust to the dark?"

"Oh, gee. I haven't heard that one in years. It's Dickinson, I think. Something about being accustomed to the dark. I can only recall the line 'as when the neighbor holds the lamp to witness her good-bye.' I know there is something about evenings of the brain, too. I've had one or two of those myself," she said ruefully.

"I hear you."

A feeble knock rattled against the door. "I'm sorry," Red said, struggling out of the overstuffed recliner, "I didn't know you were expecting company."

"No need to leave. It's Solomon. He stops by almost every day for a snack and helps me with the birds."

She ushered in a tiny child with enormous cocoa eyes and a dangerous-looking mop of black hair. He had his Giants cap wrung between his fingers, one foot hooked behind the other. The cocoa eyes were immediately fixed on the tile floor.

"Solomon, I'd like you to meet Ms. Finchley. She works for a big art gallery in New York City."

The boy mumbled something to the tiles.

"Solomon is in third grade. He is a tremendous help to me, and the birds just love him, don't they, Sol?"

More mumbling.

"I am glad to meet you," Red said, smiling. " I would love for you to show me how you take care of the birds."

Ruth led the way to the kitchen.

"Let's have our snack now, Sol, then you can give Ms. Finchley a demonstration."

With a relieved sigh, the boy clambered up onto a red stool as Ruth poured lemonade and handed around a plate of chocolate chip cookies. Wordlessly, he began wolfing them down.

Red and Ruth watched the boy surreptitiously fill his jacket pockets with two cookies he had secreted in his lap. It gave Ruth tremendous satisfaction to watch the little boy enjoy her cookies. How many batches had she made for her own son? At times it seemed like the only thing he would take from her, the only way she could show him love.

When the last of the chocolate was licked off Sol's fingers, he carefully carried the plate to the sink and rinsed out the glass.

"Go on out, Sol. We'll be right behind you." The door

slammed shut before she finished the sentence. "He's a sweetheart, but he's had a rough road. His mother is an alcoholic and vanishes every few months or so. Dad is out of the picture. I think he's hungry for more than cookies. He stores them up like he's collecting them in case the well runs dry."

Noting the concerned look on the younger woman's face, Ruth added, "He's been unofficially adopted by an absolutely stalwart woman in town. She has five children of her own, but she always has room for Sol. I'm sure Mrs. Brody supplies him with treats often; she's a wonderful baker."

"Poor guy," Red said.

"Do you have children, Red?"

"Me? No. No siblings, either. Probably a good thing from all the stories I hear about other people's family dysfunctions. I grew up with a dog, a sort of schnauzer type concoction by the name of Hubbard."

"Named after the old mother with the empty cupboard?"

"Nope, the squash. He was built like a solid little squash with legs. What about you? Do you have family in Finny?"

"I have a son," Ruth said quietly. "He's grown now, with a wife. He lives in Arizona where his wife's family owns a trucking company. He keeps the books for them."

"Do you see him often?"

"No. No. I really just get my information from the annual Christmas letter." She laughed ruefully. "We were never very close, I guess."

From the moment he was born, Bryce seemed detached from his mother, indifferent even. She remembered him scooting to the far corner of his crib, staring at her with those serious black eyes. As a toddler he was so independent, so intolerant of the physical attention she tried to shower him with. He answered her offers of help with a stern "By myself!"

When she was very tired, she wondered if she had only imagined being a mother. No, she concluded, she would have imagined it better. She would imagine her boy growing up to be a gentle, kind man, a man like Jack.

"Let's go outside. Sol really does want to show off for you, even if he doesn't have the right words to say it."

The birds were hopping from foot to foot, madly trying to snatch the stale popcorn from Solomon's hands as he stood on a chair. He conducted a wild orchestra of feathers and webbed feet, leading them from one side to the other with flying trails of popcorn.

The boy plopped onto the ground, and the birds, finally convinced that the food was gone, settled themselves around his legs, pecking each other nastily as they jockeyed for position.

"Do they actually show affection?" Red asked in amazement.

"I don't know if I would go so far as to say affection, but they tolerate humans, some more than others."

Solomon drew his finger back quickly as Rutherford bit him. He stuck it in his mouth and began stroking Zachary instead.

"You see? They will even bite the hand that feeds them." An odd smell tickled Ruth's nostrils.

A sudden darkening of the sky made them all look upward.

"What in the world is that?" Red asked, watching the drifting plume of black smoke.

"I don't know," Ruth answered. Scanning the sky, she gasped. Finny's Nose was smoking.

16

Jack thought of Lacey every time he saw barbed wire.

They had met when he visited the Funshine Travel Agency to plead for a donation for the police charity auction. She was newly transplanted to Finny from the Midwest and happy to donate a weekend trip to Half Moon Bay on behalf of Funshine. He bought her lunch to thank her. Tuna salad on wheat, no mayo.

They went out a few times. He couldn't think of anything but her most of the time, but he didn't call it love. He wasn't sure he would recognize love if it came delivered by a fat boy in a diaper with a quiver of arrows on his back.

One afternoon he got a call from her neighbor, Louella Parsons, asking him to come right away. Not red-lights-and-sirens right away, but immediately would be good.

He arrived to find Lacey straddling the top of a six-foot fence, completely tangled in the barbed wire that ran across the top of the redwood planks. She was imprisoned by a cotton sock and at intermittent intervals along her blue checked sweater. Strands of her blond hair were interwoven in the sharp prongs.

He cleared his throat, and she turned her head.

"Oh, hi, Jack. How is your day going?"

He stood there, completely unable to respond. Finally he managed a weak greeting. "Just fine, Lacey. Uh, are you having some trouble?"

"As a matter of fact, yes. I was trying to put a baby bird back in the nest, and somehow I got all tangled up.

The bird seems comfortable, though." She laughed, and he thought he had never seen anything more beautiful than this crazy woman hanging from the barbed wire.

Eventually, he got her untangled. "I'm sorry to have bothered you," she said. "I'm sure you have more important stuff to do than detangling."

She chuckled and looked at him, waiting. He just stood there. Then he couldn't stand it anymore. He grabbed her shoulders and kissed her until they both ran out of breath.

He could still feel that kiss. He could still feel everything about her: the soft skin behind her neck; her cold feet pressed against him at night; the bump on her collarbone, a souvenir of a fall from a ladder in the fourth grade. He hadn't really savored those things when she was alive, fool that he was.

He wondered when the feelings would fade. Alcohol expedited the forgetting process for a while, and though he knew it was stupid, he turned to it more and more in the months following Lacey's death. Then one night he woke after one too many to find Mr. Boo-Boo and Paul looking at him reproachfully. He had not heard Paul struggling with the bathroom door. Jack threw the soiled Batman underwear and the remaining bottles in the trash and hadn't touched another drop.

The last year was a frenetic blur, a jumble of long hours at work, psychologist appointments for Paul, frantic calls to babysitters when things came up. Lacey always told him never to leave clothes sitting in the dryer too long or they would wrinkle. That's how he was living his life, tumbling through it to avoid the damage that comes from stillness. At odd moments, memories of his past sometimes poked their way into the present. Like the amazing woman trapped in barbed wire, a woman he had taken for granted.

"Get a grip," he said, shoving the emotions back into their dark ventricle. He balled his hands into fists and squeezed his eyelids together to shut out the memories.

Work.

Stepping under the yellow tape, he entered Crew Donnelly's cottage to see if he had missed anything the last two times he'd been there.

It was hot, dank. He left the door open as he walked slowly around the tiny area. A small bed, made up neatly. A semi-enclosed kitchen with a microwave and a dorm-sized fridge. The microwave smelled like baked potatoes. The fridge held a half can of black olives, an opened Coke, and a slice of pizza on a greasy paper napkin.

The bathroom was bare; the only decoration was a dried-up plug-in air freshener shaped like a shell. Nothing in the medicine cabinet but some aspirin and toothpaste. The toothbrush was glued to the counter in a crusty plop of toothpaste.

Wandering back out into the main room, he paused. His officers had leaned the Zimmerman seascape against the back wall during their search of the place. It was gorgeous; even he could see that. Roughly textured, waves of blue-green crashing on a foggy coastline.

Gorgeous. In a room entirely void of any beauty. So what in the world was it doing here?

A huge dark figure hurled itself into the room and knocked the detective to his knees. "Get off, Boo-Boo. How do you always find me? You're supposed to be in the backyard protecting the property, you big idiot!"

The dog slobbered joyfully into Jack's ear, washing him in drool and a pungent cloud of dog aroma. "All right, you mongrel. All right." He scratched behind a ragged ear until the dog's hind leg began to keep time with the scratching.

Abruptly, the animal stood rigidly still, both ears zinging upward like radar dishes. Whirling around, he started nosing wildly at the painting, sending sprays of saliva down the surface.

"Stop it, Boo-Boo! Stop!" Jack grabbed Boo-Boo's collar and hauled him out the door, slamming it quickly. The dog started to whine and paw at the door, his nails scrabbling on the metal threshold.

Jack looked at the moist painting. Carefully he wiggled his pocketknife between the thin wooden backing and the pseudo frame holding the canvas in place. The backing soon came away, and he shined a penlight into the opening.

"Would you look at that," he said. "Maybe Lacey was right about the crazy dog after all."

That's when the acrid scent of smoke finally permeated his consciousness.

Ruth immediately sent Solomon home, and she and Red raced down the slope behind Ruth's cottage and up the wooded hillside. It seemed as though the fog was working against them, thrusting out chilled hands to prevent them from reaching the plateau. Ruth scrambled to the top minutes before her panting partner. At the apex, they were able to see clearly the orange glow coming from Prinn's greenhouse.

Clouds of black smoke swirled inside, and pockets of orange flame sprouted up here and there like a crazed monarch butterfly beating itself against the glass windows. They ran closer until they could feel waves of heat enveloping them.

"Oh no!" gasped Ruth. "I hope no one—?" The sound of exploding glass flattened them to the ground; they shielded their faces. Shards imbedded themselves into the long grass around them, and Ruth felt a prick on the back of her neck.

Several more people crested the top of the hill, and Ruth could make out Napoleon through the swirling smoke. He went from an all-out sprint to a dead stop as his greenhouse came into view.

"Those thugs!" Prinn shouted, throwing a vicious punch at no one.

He began to move toward the blazing structure. Ruth saw March put out a restraining hand. He shook her off angrily and took two more steps before a thunderous crash stopped everyone in their tracks.

Ruth and the others watched, mesmerized, as the peaked ceiling imploded with a shriek of protesting metal, raining glass down into the hellish fire.

March stared at the sight in horror, her face starkly white in the gloom. Again she reached out a trembling hand toward Napoleon, but it stayed frozen in the air, never making contact.

Randy and two men in speckled white overalls with paintbrushes still clutched in their hands jogged up to join them.

"I called 911. They should be here any minute." Randy's face looked oddly greenish in the glow. "I think we should move back in case the side walls blow out completely."

He put a hand on March's elbow and guided her away. Ruth, Red, and the painters followed. They all huddled near a stone bench, watching Napoleon silhouetted against the bonfire.

Randy looked uncertain. After a moment's hesitation he returned to his brother and spoke quietly to him from behind.

"Get away from me!" Prinn said loudly enough for all of them to hear.

The whine of a fire truck announced the arrival of the volunteer fire department. Setting up a hose line well back from the falling glass, they began a relatively futile effort to extinguish the fire. Streams of water seemed to anger it into hissing and bellowing with renewed vigor. Even Ruth's untrained eye could see there was no hope of saving the structure.

Captain Ernie Gonzalez approached Napoleon. "Mr. Prinn, is there a possibility that anyone was inside?"

Napoleon's voice was so low, Ruth almost didn't hear his reply. "I don't think so," he said dully. "Just my plants."

"Okay. I'm afraid it's pretty much a loss. We'll keep the water on it and watch the surrounding area to make sure it doesn't spread. You need to move away for your own safety." He took hold of Prinn's sleeve and gently pushed him over to a bench. "You'd better sit here until the cops arrive."

"Cops?"

"Well, clearly the thing didn't burst into flames on its own. That fire spread like butter in the sun. Some sort of accelerant. Just sit tight and wait for PD. They'll be here soon."

Ruth waited until the captain had left before she sat down next to Napoleon. She noticed a thin line of blood trickling down his forehead like a tiny wandering worm.

"You're cut. Above your eye. Do you have a handkerchief or something?"

He ignored her, staring into space.

"I am so sorry. I know how important your greenhouse was to you." She waited, her conscience battling with her curiosity, curiosity finally winning out.

"You said 'those thugs.' Do you know who set this fire, Napoleon?"

His head snapped around to fix her with an intense stare. "No. No. Of course not. I didn't say that. I must have been spouting some expletive, Ruth. You misunderstood me."

She looked at him as his gaze returned to his greenhouse, the flames dancing in the dark pools of his eyes. He looked so lost, so utterly defeated, that for a moment she had a strong urge to put her arms around him.

The strobing red and blue lights of the Finny Police Department caused them all to look up and see Jack Denny arriving, code three.

All except Napoleon Prinn, who sat and watched his greenhouse burn. Ruth had a strange feeling he wasn't thinking about his incinerated plants.

17

*S*he was halfway through. Twenty-six more pages to go. Not a bad attempt for a first-year graduate student. She was starting to add another comment in the margin when a sudden clearing of the throat nearby caused her to launch the papers into the air.

Through the blizzard of papers floating slowly to the floor, she saw a very embarrassed uniformed man, holding a white paper bag with one hand and a cowboy hat in the other, standing in the open doorway.

"I didn't mean to startle you, Professor Pena. Let me help you pick these up."

Roper Mackey dropped to his knees and began retrieving papers. She met him on the floor halfway under her desk.

"Don't worry about it. The pages are numbered," she said, pushing heavy black hair out of the way. "We only have to find the last twenty-six."

A few minutes later they both stood up. Roper banged his head as he tried to extricate his wide shoulders from underneath her desk. Sheepishly he handed her a tousled stack of papers.

"I am really sorry about that. I guess I'm about as helpful as long underwear in the desert." He paused, looking totally self-conscious, like a kid at the opera. "So, er, what are you reading about?"

"Manet," she said, plopping down into the chair again. "If you want the whole enchilada, it's 'The Function of the Picture Surface as Redefined by Edouard Manet,' but that's a mouthful."

"Er, yeah. I guess so." He cleared his throat again, softly.

"I just wanted to tell you, to say, to apologize again for my comments in the hospital. I didn't mean to sound like a chauvinist pig, but I guess that's how it came out of my big mouth. Anyway, I'm sorry for being rude."

"And for breaking my finger," she added helpfully.

"Especially for breaking your finger." He cleared his throat again. "You must be new in town. I would remember seeing you around, I think."

"I just started here two weeks ago."

"How do you like it? Georgia, I mean."

"I liked it just fine until I got mixed up in a homicide in progress."

His eyes wandered until they rested on the bag in his hand. "Oh. I brought you some carbohydrates."

She laughed and took the bag. "Mmm. Chocolate chip cookies. I may just have to forgive you after all. Thank you, Officer Mackey."

"Well now, why don't you call me Rope?"

"Okay. And you can call me Ben." Noting the strangled look on his face, she added, "Or Benjamina. That's good, too."

"That's great. I see you've got a lot of reading to do about the picture thing. I'd better let you get back to it." He hesitated, looking down at his worn boots.

"Is there anything else, Rope?"

"Well, I sort of figured, since you are new in town and all, maybe you haven't seen any of the sights. Maybe I could. . ." His voice trailed off.

She regarded him thoughtfully, the huge macho cowboy, looking remarkably like a nervous little boy. "Sure."

He looked up. "Sure?"

"Sure. I'd love to see the sights with you."

"You would? Well. You would. How about I pick you up

on Saturday? Around 1:00?"

"I have a class until 1:30."

"All right. How about two, then?" His relief was obvious as he replaced his hat and turned to leave.

"Don't you want my address?"

He paused. "Oh, right. What is your address?"

"You already know it, don't you? Along with all my other vital statistics."

He grinned. "Just one or two. See you on Saturday, Ms. Pena." She didn't correct him as he walked out the door.

This chapter was not in the notebook. At first, Ruth assumed Phillip had merely skipped a number, but she found it while cleaning out an old receipts file in the study. She sat down to read it, but her mind kept straying back to yesterday's greenhouse disaster.

She had stayed at the fire scene well into the afternoon, questioned first by Captain Gonzalez and then by Jack. The details got blurry after the fire was contained and the witnesses bustled off.

Somewhere in the midst of it all, the Finny Ladies' Organization for Preparedness arrived. Regrettably known as FLOP gals, the ladies of Finny felt it their duty and calling to provide comfort and aid of all kinds in cases of catastrophe or stress. Mrs. Florence Hodges was the figurehead of the organization, and Ruth knew her to be a woman of steely nerves. Flo believed that every catastrophe in life could be eased by a cup of steaming coffee and a triple-fudge brownie. She had shown up with both at the hospital the night Phillip had the heart attack.

The FLOP ladies arrived on scene in the middle of the melee at the greenhouse bearing coffee and treats for those watching the blazing mess. They all sat, huddled together in disbelief, munching on brownies. Napoleon stood apart, as if he were daring the fog to touch him.

Monk was there, too. He came charging up the path, puffing like a freight train. Ruth saw him seek her out, his face creased with worry. She assured him she was fine, but he put his arm around her anyway. For a few moments, she let him.

For now she put that out of her mind. The person who kept surfacing was Napoleon Prinn. "*Those thugs,*" he had said, his face a mask of rage. Why rage? Certainly shock, grief, disbelief. The one emotion that was missing was surprise.

Napoleon Prinn did not seem surprised to find his beloved greenhouse burning to the ground.

The greenhouse looked like a hideous black spider lying on its back with charred legs poking up into the air. Though it was two days after the fire, the air was still heavy with the acrid smell of old smoke. Shards of glass lent a sparkle to the scorched grass.

Inside the burned-out shell, Ernie Gonzalez was on his hands and knees, avoiding the glass as best he could. In spite of the brisk morning air, his black curly hair was dripping with sweat as he heaved his heavy torso along the ground. Behind him, in a borrowed pair of turnouts, Jack held a silver paint can in one gloved hand and a camera in the other.

"Why can't we use plastic bags, Ernie? These paint cans are a pain in the neck."

"That's why you're carrying them." Ernie stopped to peer closely at a blackened pile. "The hydrocarbons would eat right through plastic bags. Didn't you pay attention in your fire science class?"

"I must have missed that one. Are you sure about this?"

"I'd bet my new reel on it."

They peered in silence for a few minutes. "What are we looking for again?"

"You'll know it when you see it. Something out of place. Some sort of—*Aha!* What did I tell you?" He pointed to a spot just beyond a tangle of broken pots. "Get a couple of shots of that. Be sure to get a few wide shots so we can see it in relation to the windows."

Dutifully, the detective took digital pictures of the

spot Ernie was pointing to like an eager hunting dog. Gonzalez waited for Jack to finish and gingerly picked up the broken sooty bottle. There was still a fragment of blackened cloth stuffed into the mouth.

Ernie beamed like a man who had just found the Hope Diamond. He lowered it reverently into a paint can and tamped down the lid with his thumbs.

"That's it?" Jack was expecting something more dramatic.

"Whaddya mean, that's it? It's a Molotov cocktail. Pretty crude. You grab an old bottle, fill it with some sort of flammable liquid like gasoline, and add a shot of diesel. Stuff a handkerchief into the mouth, light it, and chuck it through the window. Whoosh!"

"Which window did it come through?"

"That one, I'm thinking." He pointed to what used to be the west window. "Lots of shrubs around the perimeter. Wouldn't be hard to do the deed without being seen."

They walked outside and took a few more pictures. The ground crunched underfoot as if they were walking over a bowl of Grape-Nuts.

"How long from the time it was thrown to the time you guys got here?"

"Hard to say. When we arrived it was fully involved. I'd say maybe fifteen minutes or so."

"So whoever it was had plenty of time to wander casually away. You don't think it was kids out for some fun?"

"No way to tell for sure, but doesn't feel like kids. Too much prep work involved to make a cocktail. Gotta bring the gas, rags, and stuff. Kids do dumb spur-of-the-moment stuff. This isn't where they usually come to hang out, either. If it was kids, I'll hear about it real soon.

Never met a teen who could keep their mouth shut about a thing like this for very long."

The radio on the captain's belt began to sputter.

"I gotta go. Old Mr. Deenish says there's a cobra in his backyard. I've told him a thousand times we don't have cobras here, but he couldn't tell a snake from his own garden hose. Call me if you need anything else."

He clambered into the beat-up Bronco and started the engine. Then he stopped.

"Gee whiz," Ernie said thoughtfully, "I just thought of something. This being an arson fire and all, I guess you'll be writing up the report. See you around." He drove away laughing.

Jack headed off for the gallery in search of the curator. As he entered the building, he caught sight of his face reflected in the glass. He wiped the soot off of his nose as best he could before walking to the rear of the building in search of Prinn's secretary.

"Hello, Ms. Browning."

March looked up from her papers nervously, a wave of blond hair falling into her face. "Hello, Detective." She shoved the hair back behind one ear. "What can I do for you?"

"I'd like to talk to Mr. Prinn. Is he around?"

"Well, yes. He's very busy, though. You know, dealing with the fire and the opening and everything."

He nodded pleasantly. "I'm sure he's not too busy to spare a few moments for the police, now, is he?" His casual demeanor did not hide the intensity in his eyes. He was sweaty, tired, and in no mood to be trifled with.

"Yes. I mean no. I'll see if I can get him for you." She scurried away.

The curator was sitting at his desk, thumbing through

files marked COLONIAL HOME INSURANCE. He looked up at the detective and smiled politely.

"Detective. How nice to see you. What can I do for you?"

Jack seated himself once again in the torturous brocade chair. He decided on the direct approach. "You have had a few misfortunes lately. I'm beginning to think your string of bad luck is more than a coincidence."

"Bad luck?"

"I'd say the murder of your gardener was pretty unfortunate."

"Oh yes. I expect he fell in with the wrong crowd."

"Then there's the torching of your greenhouse."

"That could have been accidental. The wiring in that place was quite old."

"More likely it was the Molotov cocktail that did it."

Prinn was silent for a while. "I can't imagine why anyone would destroy my greenhouse. It must have been vandals."

"Is the greenhouse insured?"

"As a matter of fact, no. Only the gallery proper is insured, not the greenhouse, because it was an outlying structure. No matter; it won't be that costly to replace." He spoke cheerfully.

"Who would want to burn down your greenhouse?"

"I've no idea."

"Do you have any idea why Donnelly had one of your Zimmerman paintings in his cottage before he was murdered?"

"No. I can't imagine why he would have one."

"Didn't you notice one was missing?"

"All of the artwork has been removed from the walls and put in the storage room. I had no idea any was missing.

I'll take an inventory immediately." He scribbled a note on the desktop blotter. "I didn't realize Mr. Donnelly was an art lover."

Jack smiled. "Maybe he just loved the marijuana."

Prinn started, eyes round, mouth open. "What? What did you say?"

"I said marijuana. Dried, pressed, and packaged beneath the canvas. Waiting to be shipped out, I would guess."

Prinn closed his mouth and swallowed. "Surely you aren't implying that I have anything to do with drug smuggling?"

"You housed the painting. You hired the handyman. Your greenhouse is torched. Like I said, you seem to have a really bad string of luck working here."

Napoleon sat up straight in his chair. "I house lots of paintings, Detective. That's my business. I hired Donnelly purely by chance, and as for my greenhouse, I don't know what happened to it. That is your department."

"Did you know Donnelly before you hired him?"

"No."

"Did you make several trips to New York last year?"

"Yes."

"Did you meet anyone there?"

"Of course. I met lots of people there," he snapped.

"Did you meet anyone there who was involved in the drug smuggling business?"

"Not that I'm aware of."

"Did you have any knowledge that your paintings were being used to smuggle marijuana?"

"Absolutely not."

Jack stood. "A team is on its way down here to search your storage rooms and files." He noted the belligerent look on the curator's face. "Yes, I do have a warrant."

Prinn rose and leaned over his desk, his hands like spiders on the desktop. "You see to it that they don't ruin any of my artwork," he hissed, the calm façade breaking apart like fractured glass, "—or dirty my gallery. I have an event here on Friday, and I won't let anything jeopardize that."

Jack felt the perverse thrill that often came when people pushed, mistaking his good nature for pliability. When the situation called for it, he could be as pliable as quick-drying cement.

"They will be careful, Mr. Prinn." He fixed the curator with an unblinking gaze. "And you will stay out of their way."

At the threshold he paused. "One more thing. Someone has decided to incinerate something very important to you. Seems like they're trying to send you a message. I'd listen if I were you."

On his way down the hall, Jack headed for March's office. As he approached, he heard voices coming from behind the open door.

"What did he do to make them angry?" a woman's voice said.

"I don't think it takes much to make them angry."

"What are we going to do?"

"Nothing. We just wait, like we planned. See what happens."

"Randy, I feel like this is spinning out of control. I don't want to get caught up in something bad."

"Don't worry, honey. Everything will be fine. I'm going to take care of you. I promise."

Jack walked into the office. On the other side of her desk, March and Randy stiffened, electrified.

"Detective! I didn't hear you come in. How long—what did you want?" March's face was white.

Randy regained his composure more quickly, the easy smile back in place. "Did you finish your investigation of the fire?" he asked. His hands were thrust into the pockets of his wrinkled khakis, and he leaned casually against the desk.

"Not yet. We're broadening the scope a bit. To include other things."

"Like what?" he asked. "Or is it top secret?"

"Like marijuana smuggling. You wouldn't know anything about that, would you?"

Their mouths dropped almost in unison.

"Marijuana?" March stammered. "What? In the greenhouse?"

"No. In the artwork displayed in this gallery. Did you know anything about that?"

"In the artwork? Are you kidding me? Who? Are you saying our paintings have been used to smuggle drugs?"

If she was faking complete shock, she was doing a great job of it. "Mr. Prinn denies any involvement. What do you say?"

Randy squared his shoulders. "What exactly are you accusing her of, Detective?"

"I'm not accusing her, or you, of anything. Yet. I just want to know what she knows."

"I had no idea there was any marijuana in this gallery." Her blue eyes looked straight into his, chin raised defiantly.

"How about you?" Jack gazed at Randy.

"Hey, I just came into town to write up a story on

a gallery opening. If I had known illegal substances were involved, I would be writing a much better piece, believe me."

"I see. How did you and Ms. Browning happen to meet?"

Randy gave him a knowing look. "It was entirely coincidental, you'll be disappointed to learn. We hooked up at an art convention in Mendocino last year. I had no idea she worked at my brother's gallery when I met her." He looked at her slyly. "She wasn't wearing a name tag or anything."

March's face went from white to a deep red before it settled into a rosy shade of pink. "Do you have to tell him?" she mumbled.

Randy went on. "I was there covering the event for the *Coastal Times,* and she was there scouting some new talent for my brother. Incredibly, we booked rooms right next to each other at a bed-and-breakfast. I heard a cry for help from next door and I responded code three, I think you would say in the police world. Fortunately, the door was unlocked, and I found this lovely lady in distress." He laughed.

"Well, you might as well tell him now," March said, exasperated. "I was doing some yoga in my pajamas, and I had a terrible back spasm. I couldn't even get up off the floor to grab the phone and call for help. I was stuck right in the middle of a downward dog."

She began to giggle. "He was really nice about the whole thing. He helped me up and put some ice on my back until the spasm went away. We were both surprised to learn that I worked for his brother, and I made him swear under pain of losing his liver that he would never breathe a word of our meeting, or the relationship in general, to his brother."

"Why did you want your relationship with Randy kept quiet?" Jack asked around a grin.

"I knew Napoleon couldn't stand his brother, and I figured it would only make it harder for me here."

"Right. So who were you talking about? Before I came in. Who do you think torched the greenhouse?"

March swallowed convulsively. "He is my boss, Detective." She folded her arms across her silk blouse, twining them together like wicker.

"Whatever you say to me will stay between us for the time being." He sighed and rubbed his sooty jaw. "You don't really have much choice here."

Randy and March exchanged glances. March went to the door and closed it. "I don't know what is going on. We worked so hard to build this gallery. Now what happens? The gardener is dead. Marijuana in the paintings."

She looked angry. "I have made this idiot gallery my life. I poured my heart and soul into it and not for the money, I can tell you that. And not for the gratitude, because there isn't any. We were finally getting there. Getting some recognition for quality work and the gallery itself."

She slammed both hands flat on the desk with a crack. "My parents didn't send me to college so I could wind up wasting my entire life."

Jack let her breathe heavily for a minute, while Randy gently massaged her shoulder.

"You knew something around here wasn't right. When did you realize there was a problem?"

She sank slowly back into her chair. "Look. All I know is there have been weird phone messages coming in every once in a while. They're from men. They never leave names. They just want Napoleon to call. Every time he gets a message, it scares the stuffing out of him. They don't sound like they're interested in art, you know?"

"Where do the calls originate?"

"The East Coast. New York."

"What do you think is going on?"

She shot Randy a quick look. "I thought maybe he borrowed money from the wrong people. Something like that."

"Did he come into some money recently?"

"Well, the gallery renovation wasn't cheap, and the new piece from New York was pricey. I don't keep the books, so I can't tell you how much money was involved or where it came from."

"So you figured he borrowed from the wrong guys and they've been hassling him to collect. Got it. I need to get things going. I'll be back to talk to you both again, I'm sure." He turned to go.

"Are we still going to be able to have our gallery dedication on Friday?"

"There will be a team arriving to search the gallery and offices momentarily. If they don't find anything too spicy, you can have your dedication as planned."

She sighed and nodded.

"Is there anything else you need to tell me, Ms. Browning?"

"No. What else could I tell you?"

He looked into her blue eyes and wondered the exact same thing.

Ruth sucked in the savory aromas that circled around Monk's shop. She came to deliver some brochures she had done for him, complete with photos of some of his more mouthwatering dishes. Monk wasn't there, but there was a scatter of tiny pasta on the floor. She was on her way to fetch the broom to sweep up when the bell on the door tinkled.

Ruth called out from the back storage room as soon as she heard the front door open. "Monk, is that you?" She heard scrabbling noises followed by a muffled crash as a body hit the floor.

"Oh no," Ruth cried, running to the front. "Are you hurt?" She ran over to assist the young man who was sprawled on the floor.

Monk had raced through the door just in time to see him fall. His arms were full of paper grocery sacks. Panting, he dropped the bags on the counter and knelt beside the prone figure. "Oh, for the love of lasagna. Are you all right there, fella?"

"Should I call 911?" Ruth asked.

"No need." Randy extended a shaky hand from his uncomfortable position on his back.

"Monk, this is Randy Prinn, Napoleon's brother."

"Pleased to meet you," Monk said. "Let me help you up. I should have swept that up before I left." He looked up. "Hello, Ruth. You look lovely today. I got you some onions at the Wednesday sale."

She blushed as they each took a hand and hauled Randy to his feet. "I'm really sorry, Randy," Ruth said. "I was just

120

going to get the broom when I heard you come in."

"That's quite an alarm system you got there. What is it?"

"Couscous," Monk explained. "One of the bags split and sent the buggers everywhere. I just went to get some more. You sure you aren't hurt?"

"Not hurt." He brushed the tiny pasta balls from his denim jacket and released another shower from his pant cuff. "I was taking a stroll around the main drag here and I smelled the heavenly aroma of coffee. I was wondering if you dabbled in the retail java business. I could really use a fix."

"Sure thing. It's on the house."

"Better than on the floor."

Monk went to prepare a pot of coffee, pointing to some fresh muffins for Ruth to pile on a plate.

Randy sat at a scarred table looking out at the shore. Monk plunked a steaming cup of coffee in front of him and squeezed around the other side of the table, holding his own mug. They sipped quietly for a minute, warming their hands on the mugs.

"Do you want to join us, Ruth?" Monk asked.

"No, no," she said. "I'm just going to clean up this coffee mess." The cleaning allowed her to be within comfortable earshot of the conversation.

"So you are Prinn's brother," Monk said. "If you don't mind me saying so, you're not a lot alike."

"What? I don't strike you as an obnoxious egotist? I'll take that as a compliment."

Ruth smiled to herself.

"Well, I wasn't going to insult your kin, but he does come across that way now and again."

"I know. Believe me. I grew up with him."

"Round here?"

"Down south. My father had a dental practice. Boney stayed there until he graduated, and I stayed until my parents died."

"Oh. Sorry to hear that. Accident?"

"I guess you could say that. Dad had a few too many at the club and gassed an old lady during a gum-planing procedure. She died. The malpractice suit pretty much ruined them both."

He stretched his long legs under the table. "Dad had a heart attack, and Mother died six months later of a stroke. I think it was more from shame than arteries. Her socialite friends cut her out like a patch of Ebola."

"No wonder Napoleon has such an unusual personality, with that family life," Ruth muttered to herself.

"Well, that is a spot of bad luck," Monk said. "Must have broken you up pretty good."

Randy shrugged. "Actually, it wasn't too bad for me. Took away some of the pressure."

"How do you mean?"

"Oh, I was the proverbial black sheep for reasons too numerous to mention, so I felt compelled to try and find something I was really good at. You know, unloved kid tries to win parents' approval."

Randy put down his mug and shoved his thumbs into the belt loops of his worn jeans. "Maybe it's because we're twins: Boney and I did everything more or less at the same time, in the same location. I was a flop in school. I decided to become an athlete, but as it turns out, you actually have to be good at sports to succeed in that career. Then I decided my real talent must be writing. What about you? You have family here?"

"Not here. Mom and Pop live in Kansas. Both in their nineties and still running a ranch, although my brother does most of the heavy stuff now."

"And you didn't get the ranching bug?"

"Nah. You ever been to Kansas? All it is, is a lot of flat surrounded by a lot more flat. I couldn't wait to get out. The navy was the perfect answer for me."

"Did you retire?"

"I took an early retirement." Monk folded his hands across his rounded belly and stared absently up at the overhead lights. "The navy has changed a lot since the dark ages when I enlisted. Now the newbies are young bucks with college and computers under their belts. And then they started letting women aboard." He shot a quick look at Ruth.

"Don't worry, Monk," she said, "I know you are a closet chauvinist."

Randy laughed. "It's a whole new world, my friend, especially where women are concerned."

"You attached?"

"Nope. I hardly know a soul in town."

Hmmm. He seemed to know March pretty well, Ruth thought.

"Say, that was some fire the other night," Monk said. "What's the scuttlebutt around the gallery?"

Randy took a swig of coffee before answering. "The detective on the case is sure it's arson, but no word about any suspects that I know of. Arson's not as bad as the Mary Jane, I guess."

"Who's Mary Jane?" Ruth could not resist asking.

"That's marijuana. Apparently someone has been smuggling it in Napoleon's paintings."

Ruth's jaw hit her clavicles. "You're kidding."

"There's quite a scheme afoot, according to Detective Denny." He drained the rest of his mug. "I guess I have to go face the big bad world, but it's a lot less bad with a cup of joe under my belt. Thanks."

"No problem," Monk said. "I'd better get to it, too. I've got crab cakes to fry, and crab waits for no man."

"I'll take your word for it. Thanks for the coffee and chitchat. I'll come back for some couscous when you cook up a batch."

Randy left. Though Monk seemed composed, Ruth could tell he was as shocked by the information as she was.

"Can you imagine Napoleon involved in smuggling?" he asked.

"No," she said slowly, remembering Randy and March together in whispered conversation, "but I wouldn't rule out his brother."

20

The door to Jack's office opened and a tired-looking Nathan Katz entered. Nathan's permanently somnolent demeanor was largely due to the fact that he had five children, including triplet girls entering their threes. Sometimes tired gave way to completely exasperated, but today tired was winning.

"Give me some good news, Nate."

"The hole in the ozone layer seems to be stabilizing."

"Funny. Try again."

"It's almost Friday?"

"That's not very encouraging to a guy who works weekends." He paused for half a minute before adding, "Do you know your mustache is sparkling?"

The officer slumped dejectedly into a chair, huffing into his bushy mustache. "I know. It's Glitter 'n' Go cheek powder. The stuff is there forever; I've even tried paint thinner. I think it's the same glop they use to glue 747s together."

"You fell asleep in front of the TV again, didn't you?"

"Yeah. Iva Marie got me. Pretty stealthy for a three-year-old—I didn't feel a thing. I'm pretty sure she's got a good pick-pocketing career ahead of her."

Jack laughed. "Okay, Tinkerbell. Talk to me."

"We combed the place, Jack. Nothing. No drugs, no drying or packaging materials. The paintings are clean, and so is the gallery from what we can tell."

"Phone records?"

Nate looked at his notes. "In the past six months the gallery received four New York calls from public phones.

He didn't return any of them, at least not from a gallery phone. He made several calls to the Shaum Gallery, and they returned them. No reason to believe it wasn't legit business."

"What about the books?"

"Everything looks fine, but we made copies. No unusual deposits of money or regular withdrawals of significant sums. Of course, if he is getting some cash from an unsavory source, it isn't likely he's going to keep a record of it."

Jack sighed and leaned back in his chair. "So we have nothing to tie him to the dope."

"What about Donnelly? You get anything on him?" Katz cracked open a bottle of water that the detective handed him.

"Nothing new. Busted for possession. Small-time stuff. He only did a couple of months. He seems to have stayed out of trouble, at least until he landed in our quiet little hamlet."

"Maybe he planted the dope." Nate swigged down some water.

"It's possible. But why use a Zimmerman painting? And where did he get such a quality stash? That is some excellent weed, to quote the lab boys. Why can't we find the connection here?"

Nate drained the water bottle and slam-dunked it in the trash can. "Oh yeah. One more thing. Mary accidentally knocked an ashtray thingy over when we were searching the storeroom. Only it wasn't an ashtray; it was some work of art or something. Prinn says you owe him eight hundred bucks."

"I should have been an orthodontist," Jack said to the closing door.

When Ruth arrived at the door of the gallery Friday evening, she was impressed at the immaculate paint and the burnished brass doorknobs, highlighted by the footlights at each side of the cement steps. No one would ever guess there had been a fire only two hundred yards away now that the setting sun concealed the blackened greenhouse beams.

A tall teenage girl greeted her warmly. "Hi, Mrs. B. How are those birds?"

Lizzie Putney was a high school student who had worked for a while at Phillip's veterinary clinic. Ruth eyed the row of hoops twining down the girl's left ear and connecting via a delicate chain to a hoop in her nostril.

"Hi, Lizzie." She wrapped the girl in a hug. "You look. . .great," said Ruth, shifting her camera bag to the other shoulder.

"I'm helping out Monk tonight with the food. Don't I look the part?" She minced along for a few steps. "I'll show you to the dining hall, my lady."

Ruth gave her a squeeze. "Thank you. And how is your menagerie?" The girl had, at last count, four turtles, six cats, a one-eyed frog named Nelson, and an ancient guinea pig fondly referred to as "the old geezer." As a much younger child, she had soberly lugged each unfortunate critter to Mr. Budge for medical advice.

"Oh, they're all fine." She giggled. "But my dad says I had better come up with a plan before I go away to college. He says he isn't Dr. Doolittle." She giggled again as she led the way into the large foyer. "See you later, Mrs. B. I gotta go be couth!"

Ruth wondered if couth and nose rings were compatible.

The room was sparkling with white linens and candles twined with garlands of white roses and ivy. Prinn had class, no doubt about it. She took out her camera and snapped a few shots of the pristine dining tables. A few people were milling about, and she took their pictures, too.

Maude Stone was standing with Flo Hodges, pointing at a watercolor. She wore navy blue from head to toe with a matching feathered hat. Flo burst into loud peals of laughter at some comment from Maude.

Nestled in an inconspicuous corner of the foyer was the catering headquarters, and looking supremely conspicuous in a chef's white togs was Monk. He snapped off a jaunty salute with his slotted spoon and plunged it into a steaming stockpot. Her heart beat faster as she approached.

"That smells divine, Monk."

"Thankee, ma'am." He lowered his voice conspiratorially. "The little weasel ordered me not to associate with the guests, but I won't turn down a compliment from such a gorgeous lady. Is this place duded up or what?"

She blushed, looking around the foyer and beyond, into the adjoining corridor. There was a movement of shuffling people. More guests were arriving. Bubby Dean looked uncomfortable in a too-tight blazer. He waved at her, and she waved back. She guessed Alva had not been invited since he was not standing at the hors d'oeuvres table stuffing his pockets.

She whispered a good-bye to Monk and made her way past cushioned chairs to the displays of art. Her eyes were drawn to the soft watercolors. Foamy waves, peaceful gulls bobbing gracefully on gray water. Ha! Nothing like her family of squabbling children, fighting to the death over a stale muffin.

Farther down the hallway were reproductions of various well-known paintings and sculptures. The rest of the gallery was devoted to watercolors, oils, and the occasional sculpture, all done by coastal artists. Ruth knew enough to recognize that Napoleon had an exceptional eye.

She spotted Randy's curly head bent in deep conversation with someone she did not at first recognize. As the lady threw back her head to laugh, Ruth identified Summer Sawyer. She was wearing a very tight, very black sheath dress with enough of a plunge to display plenty of skin.

Summer laid a hand on Randy's arm and caressed it.

"I wouldn't know about that," Randy was saying. "I'm only a lowly reporter with no ambition to be anything else."

A rapid staccato of high heels announced March Browning's approach. She looked so different that Ruth had to glance again to be sure. March had quite literally let her hair down, and the cascade of blond waves settled around her face like a sigh. Her blue eyes mirrored the deep cobalt of her satin dress. She was lovely, and Ruth was surprised she had not noticed it before.

"Hello, Ms. Sawyer," March said icily, pushing past her to take Randy's arm. "I see you've met my fiancé, Randy. And this is our resident photographer, Ruth Budge."

If Summer was surprised to hear about Randy's premarital status, she gave not the slightest indication of it. She nodded casually and tossed the hair back out of her face.

"Yes. We were just getting acquainted. We're both twins, so we have a lot in common." Her black eyes rested completely on him without a glance at March. "My brother is a doctor."

"Does he practice in the area?" March asked.

"No. He moved to Arizona to be nearer to my mother after my father left. Doug works on an Indian reservation somewhere in the desert. He is the great protector to his adoring tribe, my mother included."

Summer shrugged her slender shoulders. "Don't mind me. I'm just being catty. My brother really is a doll; I've worshipped him my whole life. He says it's his calling to heal people. The amazing thing is, he really believes that." She addressed her next comment to Randy. "So I guess we have something in common. We both have high-achieving brothers."

March spoke through gritted teeth. "How nice of you to come tonight, Ms. Sawyer, even though Mr. Prinn wasn't able to show your students' work."

A glint of anger surfaced in Summer's eyes. "It wasn't a problem. I know Mr. Prinn will come around eventually."

"I'm sure. Randy, I need to discuss a few things with you. Excuse us, won't you, Ms. Sawyer?"

Summer nodded smoothly. "Of course. I was just going to find another Perrier anyway. I'll be seeing you soon." She walked gracefully toward the bar. Ruth was just about to edge away as quietly as she had come when Randy took her arm.

"Mrs. Budge, you look fabulous. The eyebrows are coming along."

March said acidly, "He inherited some of the Prinn charm, don't you think, Ruth? All the lovely ladies seem to think so." She stiffly pulled away from him.

"Are you going to unveil the new piece for us?" Ruth asked.

"I think Mr. Prinn would not appreciate me stealing his thunder."

"If you don't mind my asking, why didn't Napoleon want to show the work from Summer's college?"

March grimaced. "He said the work was fine at first, but then he changed his mind. He said it was juvenile."

"Was it?"

"As much as I hate to admit it, I thought the work was quite good." She lowered her voice and leaned closer. "I think what it really came down to is that she told him his "new addition" wasn't worth the price he paid for it. He doesn't like to be made a fool of. He ruined her chances of moving up in the university, I think." There was a tiny smile of satisfaction on March's face.

"She's definitely a woman who knows what she wants," Randy said thoughtfully.

"I have some things to check on. I will talk to you later." March gathered her skirts and walked away in an angry hiss of satin.

"If you'll excuse me, I think I'd better go smooth some ruffled feathers." He started off after her.

"Ah, there you are, Mrs. Budge. I was afraid you had gotten a better invitation."

"Hello, Napoleon."

He took her elbow and steered her toward a small cluster of people. "Come over here and mingle. You'll have a perfect view. I will get started shortly."

Ruth kept her head low in an effort to avoid Maude. She found herself standing next to the rumpled Buster Dent and his daughter. Dimple looked like a little woodland elf in a green silk shift. Her hair was twisted in a loose braid, and tendrils floated down her full cheeks. Buster appeared to be a shade short of furious, his weathered skin pulled into angry puckers around his eyes.

"Hello, Mr. Dent. Are you here to admire the new acquisition?"

"I've already seen the ugly thing. It surely ain't worth thirty grand," he growled. Beads of sweat shone on his upper lip. He had made an honest attempt to spruce up for the evening, plastering his white hair into a sort of hirsute halo and changing his flannel shirt and jeans for polyester pants and a wide striped tie.

"So you've seen it, then?" Ruth pried.

"Seen it? I practically bought the piece of junk."

"Why don't you like it?"

He glowered at her for a moment, his face so close to hers she could smell the shrimp puffs on his breath. "I guess it doesn't matter, now, does it? He doesn't need my approval, just my money."

A nasally voice crept into the conversation. Wanda stood close by with arms crossed, a shiny-headed man slightly behind her.

"I just cannot fathom what is happening to our gallery. What will become of our local artists if we begin importing talent?"

"I don't know, Wanda. Have your paintings been displaced?" Ruth asked.

Her face flushed. "Of course not. They are displayed on the north wall, there. They have to be grouped thematically, you know, since the focal point of this room is apparently sculpture now."

"Apparently. Where is Bun tonight?"

"Oh, she can't make it to these evening functions. It's way too tiring for her."

Ruth nodded as she watched Napoleon mount the

dais and clear his throat.

"Welcome. I am so pleased to see you all here this evening to witness a triumph for the Finny Art Gallery. As you well know, it has been my mission since the inception of this gallery ten years ago to represent the finest artists in the region. I believe I can say, with all modesty, that that mission has been accomplished."

As the curator droned on, Ruth edged to the side and aimed her camera at the crowd. Randy lounged indolently against an oak beam, a pencil projecting from behind his ear. March drummed nervously on a glass in her hand.

The man Ruth remembered as Buck Pinkey positively shone as he sipped Perrier.

"The new addition marks a turning point for this gallery. Instead of limiting our works to coastal artists, we will now be representing important works from all over the country. The first is a sculpture from the artist Carmine.

"Somewhat of a mysterious fellow, he has never attended any showing of his work and remains elusive, preferring to stay in the shadows. His work is praised for its luminous quality and perfect balance of line and contour. He is a sculptor in the purest sense. His works are few and highly sought after, and it is with great pride that I present to you the new addition to our gallery, entitled *Broken Bird*."

With a flourish, he whisked the white canvas from the shoulder-high statue.

The room was buried in complete silence.

Gradually, low murmurs and the hum of quiet conversation filled the void. Wielding her camera and elbows, Ruth made her way to the platform, squeaking past Red. Her breath caught in her throat.

The raw emotion of the piece stunned her. The figure was a young child. A naked girl, crouching, crumpled in agony. In her outstretched hands a lifeless bird lay, limp wings draping over her slender fingers.

The statue was marble, and the girl's face seemed almost to shine with the bitter tears coursing down her cheeks. Amazed at the captured emotion, she managed to get one shot of the piece before she tore her eyes away.

"Oh brother," Wanda said. "This is it? The great gift to our local art world? How completely maudlin." Spotting Red nearby, she went on. "This is the great work from the Shaum Gallery? Really, I've seen better in park fountains."

"Yeah?" Bubby said, stuffing a shrimp into his mouth. "Looks okay to me. I kinda like it."

"You would," Maude said.

Red narrowed her eyes as Wanda continued.

"Art isn't your business, Bubby. Tourists are not going to come to Finny and take home a thing like that in their suitcases."

"Do you sell to a lot of out-of-towners?" It was Buck.

"I sure do. I've sold six just this month. People come here especially to find my work. They don't need to have a fancy piece from New York to impress the neighbors. My clients have good sense."

Ruth could see Red stiffen.

"I suppose it would be possible for me to care less, but I'd really have to work at it," Red said quietly.

Wanda stared at her, unable to comprehend what she had just heard. *"What?"*

Bubby must have sensed a storm brewing. "I'm going

to get some more of those crab thingies." He moved away.

Red replied slowly, fiercely. "What gives you the right to pass judgment on this sculpture—or any other piece for that matter? What do you actually know about art, anyway? Or do you just parrot the ignorance around you?"

"Who are you calling ignorant?" Buster's face was starting to mottle. His calloused hands were balled. "Just because you work for some fancy city art gallery don't make you the skin on the cream, lady."

Napoleon, who was across the room talking to Maude and Flo, looked over at the raised voices.

"Spare me the country witticisms," ordered Red. "None of you knows the most infinitesimal thing about art." She folded her arms and regarded the oils on the far side of the room.

"You should be careful about those generalities, you know." Summer looked over the rim of her glass as she settled gracefully onto a padded bench.

March hurried over, a worried crease in her brow. "Ms. Finchley, would you care to pose for a picture in front of *Broken Bird* since you brought it to our gallery?"

Ruth readied her camera. Unfortunately, the intervention didn't distract Wanda. "How dare you!" she spat. "I happen to be an artist. My work brings in thousands. I haven't seen any of your work on the walls, you cretin."

"Wanda, why don't we go and get you a drink?" March said more desperately.

Red replied coolly, "I haven't seen any of yours, either. Why don't you just fess up? Tell them the truth."

"What truth?" Wanda spat.

"Tell them that you aren't the person who painted these pictures."

21

If ever there was a palpable silence, Ruth thought, this was it. You could probably suck it up with a straw. Napoleon finally disengaged himself from Maude and hurried over to the brewing crisis.

All eyes were focused on Wanda, who stood with her mouth so far ajar that her silver fillings winked in the overhead lighting. When nothing commenced from her mouth, four sets of eyes shifted to her accuser.

"I hope everyone is enjoying the evening," Napoleon said.

"I'm enjoying it a lot more now," Maude said.

Mr. Pinkey masticated a piece of ice in little staccato bursts. "Wanda didn't paint these pictures? That's a pretty strong statement, Ms. Finchley." He pulverized some more before swallowing. "Got anything to back it up?"

She strode to a huge oil framed in silvered wood. Sweeping her hand from side to side, she said, "Just look closely at the impasto."

Ruth had a fleeting thought about an hors d'oeuvre she had seen demonstrated on the cooking channel. "What exactly is—?"

Red snorted. "Impasto. Thickly applied paint. It can be done with a brush or applied right out of the tube." She looked at the blank faces. "Like Van Gogh. Stand up close and you can see the ridges and channels in the paint. This oil was done with lots of tube application and minimal brushwork. Look at the sweeping arcs from the bottom up and to the right."

"I don't think this is the time. . ." Napoleon began.

The group leaned forward and collectively wrinkled their noses, Magoo-like, at the canvas. Summer stayed where she was, unruffled.

"I see what you mean, but I don't know why that proves Wanda didn't paint them," Randy said.

"Because she's left-handed. This paint has been applied by a right-handed person. Follow the channels in the paint from the darker spot where it was squeezed from the tube upwards as the artist smoothed it with his fingers. They all flow from bottom left to top corner right. Besides, sculptured nails? There's no way you can do impasto from the tube and have Barbie doll nails like hers." She rounded on Wanda. "I'll give you credit, though. You did sign the painting. That's your signature, isn't it? At least you contributed something."

Wanda made a sound akin to the air leaking slowly from a balloon as she slid to the floor at the foot of the painting.

The small group of people progressed from stunned immobility to comic book action. March rushed to the dais and asked the guests to gather for another round of thank-yous and small talk before they had a chance to notice the chaos brewing in the corner. She successfully drew the majority of the people away from the stricken woman. Ruth and Buster raised Wanda's head and patted her hands until her eyelids fluttered open. Her mouth opened and closed like a grounded fish gasping for air.

Red laughed harshly and left, followed by Summer Sawyer.

"Wanda, can you hear me? It's Ruth."

"I think she's out of it," Buster commented gruffly.

"Maude, Flo, please go get some water," Ruth said.

Though Maude looked dismayed at having to leave the scene of the drama, she followed Flo out of the room.

"Imagine that," Buck Pinkey said, peering closely at the painting and ignoring the body underneath it. Napoleon grasped him by the arm and, with a backward glance at Wanda, drew him away down the hall. "I'll be right back," he called over his shoulder.

Wanda was the color of Wonder Bread. "I can't believe it. Who would say such things? All lies. Slander. I hope you all realize. . ." With Randy struggling under one arm and Buster under the other, Wanda was deposited on a padded bench, her body propped against a nearby ficus.

A half hour later the company straggled toward the tingling dinner bell. The ambiance was romantic, soft candlelight playing over the pristine linens. The scent of roses hung in the air and mingled with the tantalizing aroma of seafood and garlic. Everything from salad forks to sugar tongs was arranged with meticulous attention.

The dining hall should have been a gentle billow of people sipping beverages and chatting as they settled into plush chairs.

It wasn't.

Ruth was seated at a corner of the rectangular table, between Buster and Wanda. The sound of Buster's teeth grinding set hers on edge. Wanda sat silently in her place, staring at the goblet in front of her, a ficus leaf spinning crazily from a strand of hair.

"Are you sure you're feeling all right, Wanda?" Ruth asked. "I'd be happy to drive you home."

"I am fine, and no two-bit tramp from the big city is going to push me out of this party," she hissed.

Across the table was an empty chair. Ruth tried to appear inconspicuous as she eavesdropped on Randy and March, their heads bent close together. It seemed like a fairly serious conversation, and she couldn't make out a single word of it. After a moment, March excused herself and glided away.

No sign of Napoleon or Buck Pinkey. Dimple was missing, as well.

Bubby shoved a napkin down the front of his shirt and looked around hopefully for food. Maude rolled her eyes and turned her back on him.

Red sat down with arms folded and leaned back in her chair, watching Summer talk into a cell phone the size of a pack of Juicy Fruit, the hint of a smile playing over her glossy lips.

A metallic crash caused those seated at the table nearest the catering station to jump. "I can't hold dinner interminably!" Monk growled, each syllable rising in volume. "This crab bisque is ready *now*."

Another crack with the now-dented ladle sent Bert Penny hurrying to deliver steaming plates to the guests. Lizzie ran from place to place, refilling water glasses. The strained conversations gave way to contented munching as the diners enjoyed warm, pillowy sourdough rolls.

As the last bits of crusts were being devoured, March stepped to the middle of the room and tapped on a water glass. "Um, ladies and gentlemen. Er, thank you for coming tonight. Enjoy your dinner." She retreated quickly to her chair and sat down.

"Wow. Do you think she writes her own material?" Summer asked.

"I liked it," Bubby said, his mouth full of bread. "Short and sweet."

"Typical." Maude snorted.

Ruth glanced at the clock. Eight thirty-five. Tardiness was definitely not a Napoleonic trait. She dipped her spoon into the creamy saucer and inhaled deeply. She was amazed to discover that her appetite had returned. Was it the delicious food or the simmering intrigue that whetted her hunger?

Heavenly. The soup was creamy and peppered throughout with succulent chunks of crab. Ruth thought Monk had to have some divine powers lurking in that sturdy body. Wait a minute though. There was definitely a shell of some sort grating against her spoon.

No, not a shell. Gingerly, she fished around and carefully removed the foreign object. A bisquey set of keys dangled from her spoon.

She momentarily froze, watching the bisque dripping off of the keys into her bowl. Buster and Wanda both stared at her, their own spoons suspended in midair.

"Well, it's better than finding a thumb," Maude said.

Several things happened simultaneously. The keys continued to drip as they dangled from her fork. March shot to her feet as if her knees were spring loaded. Red began to laugh, and Dimple entered the dining hall and began to warble.

The warbling soon eclipsed the other details as it escalated into a shriek and resolved itself into a spectacular keening that echoed off the overhead lighting and bounced from goblet to goblet.

It ended abruptly as Dimple's head sagged forward and she fell to the floor, her head coming to rest squarely on Wanda's foot.

Wanda reflexively jerked her foot away as if she had encountered dog excrement, causing Dimple's head to thunk on the hardwood floor. "Hey! What is going on here?"

Randy knocked over his chair as he ran to the fallen woman and gently felt for a pulse. "I think she's fainted. I'm sure she wasn't aiming for your shoes, Ms. Zimmerman." He muttered, "Another one bites the dust."

Wanda backed nervously away as Monk joined Randy to examine the fallen girl. Buster pushed through the group to pat the back of her hand awkwardly. "She's never fainted before. Musta got too overheated."

"It seems to be going around tonight," Maude said.

Dimple's eyelids began to flutter, and the keening started again.

"Heee'ss—heee's—"

"I think she's saying something about cheese," Bubby stage-whispered.

"Not cheese, you moron. Why would she be talking about cheese?" Buster shouted.

"Heeee's—bleeding—I—" Her head thunked the floor again.

"Oh, for goodness' sake, will someone keep her head from hitting the floor every two minutes?" March stood at Dimple's feet, her fingers twisted together in an intricate fleshy pretzel. "What is she talking about?"

"I don't think she's coherent," Summer said, peering over the huddled shoulders in front of her. "She sounds delusional, or does she always sound like that?"

"March, call 911," Randy ordered, wiping the sweat off his forehead. "She doesn't seem to be coming around."

"You could put her on the bench near the ficus," Red piped up. "I think it's still warm."

"I don't know why," Randy said slowly, catching Monk's eye, "but I've got a strange feeling we ought to have a look down the hallway she just visited."

Monk nodded. "I think you may be right. Let's go."

Randy handed the cloth to March, and she and Buster knelt beside the tiny bundle on the floor. Ladle in hand, Monk led the way like a drum major marching through a firing range.

After depositing the keys in a napkin and stuffing them in her pocket, Ruth trailed behind them. Her head did not want to know what lay at the end of the hallway, but apparently her feet did, because they followed along in spite of some intellectual objections.

The hallway had doors opening on each side, leading to two storage rooms on the left and offices on the right. They headed immediately for the only door that was ajar, Prinn's office.

Being a step or two behind the men, Ruth did not hear their synchronized gasps. She added her own seconds later.

Napoleon was indeed in his office, and he had a very good excuse for being late for dinner.

He was wearing the remains of a ceramic pot on his head, the broken rim hanging crazily over one eyebrow. His upper body leaned against the front of the mahogany desk, and his legs were twisted under him.

Ruth was awed by the sheer amount of blood that covered Napoleon Prinn in a satiny sheet and saturated the plush mauve carpeting, creating a fantastic black whorled pattern spreading out from underneath him. Here and there tendrils of a delicate flowering plant dotted his tuxedo, and plops of soil made grainy islands in the mess.

His eyes were open and staring, seemingly fixed on the branch that appeared to spring directly from between his eyes. Still trapped in her out-of-body mode, Ruth's brain registered the comic quality to the situation, but her stomach was less than amused.

She bent over the nearby Persian throw rug and threw up.

Ruth had never noticed before that her shoes needed polishing. Now that she was sitting on a chair in the gallery foyer with her head between her knees, the scuffs on her genuine imitation leather pumps cried out for attention. She felt as though she might be screaming, but she realized the shrieks were only in her mind.

When she thought her head was whirling less aggressively, Ruth ventured to poke her head upward, turtle-like.

Things were strange. Surreal.

Two medics were loading Dimple onto a stretcher, Buster bobbing up and down behind it. She could see the top of Dimple's curly head and one of her pale hands peeking out from under the yellow blanket.

Another stretcher was lying idle in the hall, a black zippered bag neatly folded on top, waiting for another passenger. Ruth swallowed hard, blinking against the memory of Napoleon lying in a wash of blood and plant.

She noticed Detective Denny, which made her feel more secure. He was listening intently to a seated March, whose hands were clutched. Randy stood across the room watching her. They both looked wild-eyed.

The two young participants, Lizzie and Bert, were huddled together, eagerly awaiting their brush with law enforcement.

"What are you saying? Are you saying he was killed? Murdered?" Wanda sprang up from her seat across from Officer Katz so suddenly she knocked the notebook out of his hand. "I know. It was that Finchley woman. She did it."

Nate urged Wanda back into her seat. "What makes you say that, Ms. Zimmerman?"

Her glance darted around the room. "She is a troublemaker. Coming here from New York, spreading lies about my work and bragging about her high-end gallery in New York. I bet she was having an affair with him or something."

The word "affair" caused everyone to stop their conversations and look up.

Red entered the room just then, accompanied by a uniformed Mary Derisi. She glanced at Wanda. "Would you like me to write out a confession and then you can sign your name to it? You could take credit for that, too."

Before Wanda could launch herself off the bench, Nate grabbed her arm and replanted her while Mary steered Red to a seat in the far corner of the room.

A hand squeezed Ruth's shoulder, startling her. Monk bent over her, his eyes crinkled in concern. "Are you all right? I didn't realize you were behind us. It was a terrible thing to come upon."

"Yes. I think I'm better now. Did I really throw up all over the crime scene?"

"Well, yes. But I'm sure it's happened before. Got a little queasy myself. Haven't felt that way since the boiler blew on our ship and took two of our boys with it. What a thing." He sat down next to her, still holding the dented ladle.

Jack exchanged a few words with Officer Katz before approaching Ruth and Monk. "Quite an evening for you," he said. "I need to ask you a few questions before you can get out of here, I'm afraid. Feeling better?"

She nodded, blushing.

"What exactly made you two go looking for Mr. Prinn in the first place?"

Monk tapped the ladle thoughtfully on his leg. "First off, I was waiting for him to get his behind seated so we could serve dinner. We had agreed on eight o' clock sharp, and that's when the food was ready. You know when you're dealing with a bisque you can't just let it sit around for a couple of hours. If the cream boils—"

Jack interrupted the culinary tangent. "Okay, you needed to get dinner rolling—what next?"

"I sent Bert to look for Prinn out in the gallery, but he couldn't find him. Then Dimple came in and started screaming. We figured something was up."

"She entered from the rear door?"

"Yes. Saying something about blood."

"Is that what you heard, Ruth?"

"Yes, something like 'He's bleeding.' I don't know why I followed along behind Randy and Monk. I wish I hadn't now." She closed her eyes and shuddered, bile rising in her throat.

"We're almost done here. I understand there was a confrontation between Wanda Zimmerman and Red Finchley. Can you tell me what you heard?"

She retold the ugly argument. "Have you talked to Wanda about it?"

"Sure have. She denies any wrongdoing, says Ms. Finchley is some kind of, what did she say? White trash. According to the interviews I've done so far, the argument was witnessed by you, Randy, Buster, and Summer Sawyer."

"And Mr. Pinkey," Ruth added.

He looked up sharply. "Who?"

"Buck Pinkey. He's visiting here from—somewhere.

I ran into him as he left the gallery one day. He asked me about renting Crew Donnelly's place. Did you meet him, Monk?"

"No. I can't recall anyone by that name."

Jack was speaking quietly into a radio. "What does he look like?"

"Nicely dressed. Thick around the middle. Short, about my height. His eyes are. . .dark. Mostly I noticed his bald head. It's sort of speckled like a gull's egg. And shiny." She felt foolish.

He murmured into the radio again. "Where did everyone go after the argument?"

"I don't know really. We all just kind of wandered away. March tried to lure most folks at the other end of the room. Wanda said she wanted us to leave her alone. Napoleon and Buck went off somewhere, I think. I didn't keep track of everyone."

"Was anyone missing from the table after the dining hall was seated?"

"Well, Napoleon of course. Dimple. March entered a few minutes after I sat down. Red and Buster were seated when I got there. Come to think of it, I never did see Mr. Pinkey sit down. I wonder what happened to him?"

"I wonder," Jack said. Officer Katz approached, looking deadly serious, though the tract lighting encouraged a definite sparkle in his mustache. He mumbled a few words into the detective's ear.

"Okay," he sighed, "I'm going to release these folks now. Make sure we've got everyone's contact info and send them home. Meet me at the ER in twenty." The officer nodded and left.

"Monk, we're still printing and photographing everything, so I'm going to have to send you home without your equipment. It's a shame, too. The soup smells excellent. What is it? Chowder?"

"Bisque. Crab bisque."

Bisque! She stood up with a jerk and patted her pockets. "Here. I completely forgot I found these in my bowl of bisque." She handed the detective a wadded-up napkin with the keys bunched inside.

"What is that?" Monk's jaw fell open in shock. "How did those get in my bisque?"

She shrugged helplessly, feeling somehow responsible for the offending hardware.

Monk's outraged grunting overlapped the detective's chuckle. "This story gets weirder by the minute," Jack said, poking at the sticky keys with a ballpoint pen.

"If it was a novel, I wouldn't pay a nickel for it." Ruth shouldered her camera bag and heaved herself homeward, hoping the chilly walk would clear her mind.

Eden Hospital was a very familiar place to Ruth Budge. There was Phillip's fishhook-in-the-thumb trip. Her fall off the porch steps after tripping over a greedy bird. The birth of her son and the death of her husband. Everything seemed to culminate here.

She hadn't even made it home after the gallery fiasco. Something pulled her to the hospital. Concern for Dimple? Perhaps an unwillingness to face her empty house after the horrific evening, to spend the long hours listening to nothing. She knew that one word from her and Monk would hold sentry on her couch, but she just couldn't ask another man into Phillip's house. Yet.

Choosing not to dwell on motivation, Ruth headed toward the emergency room only to learn that Dimple was already scanned, medicated, and bundled off to a room on the second floor.

She padded down the tiled hallway, following the green arrows directing her to the even-numbered rooms. The door to room 214 was open. In the doorway was a doctor, Jack, and Buster. The doctor was speaking in the quiet, measured way professional people do when they are speaking to hysterical people. She inched closer, unsure whether to retreat or announce her presence with a timely cough.

"She's going to be fine, Mr. Dent; they both are. There is no evidence of a concussion, just a nasty bang to the head. She is resting comfortably now."

Both? Who else was injured at the gallery? She lost the next few sentences until Buster's voice worked its way up to shouting level.

". . . is going on? You must be wrong. Those tests are wrong!"

The detective raised a calming hand and ushered the threesome into the hallway. "Mr. Dent, just calm down."

"You calm down! I can't believe what he's saying about my daughter. I ought to crack you a new—"

Jack's calming hand became a restraining one. "That's enough. I know this is hard for you to hear. Facts are facts, and doing something stupid is not going to change anything." He turned to the doctor. "Can I talk to her now?"

"I don't think that is advisable. She's been through some trauma, and the best thing for her and the baby is rest. Come back in the morning, Detective."

Not wanting to be caught eavesdropping, Ruth scurried away, taking the stairs two at a time.

Out in the parking lot, she sat down on a cement

planter to assimilate. So Dimple was pregnant. It wasn't a disaster of epic proportions; the girl was in her twenties, not a teenager. All the same, she felt terrible for her. The prayer came out before she thought about it. "God, please watch over Dimple and her baby. Help them know they are not alone." It felt good to pray for someone else. It eased her heart for a moment. She wondered why her prayers hadn't lessened her own sense of loss.

Then her mind filled with questions again.

Who was the father? She had never seen Dimple with anyone at all.

Wait a minute. She flashed back to Dimple sitting on the steps of the gallery. Then again to the scent of roses that clung to Napoleon as he passed her on the path to the greenhouse.

"He can be temperamental, you know," she had said.

Ruth clapped a hand to her forehead.

The gunning of a motor made her jump. A car peeled out of a parking space, running up onto the curb before correcting itself. The driver stopped for a second and glared into the rearview mirror before roaring off in search of the exit.

An overwhelming feeling of déjà vu swept over Ruth. That day in the woods, when Ruth and Dimple had almost been run down.

It was the same car and the same furious driver.

Buster Dent.

Ruth watched the waves crash angrily against the shore, sending spray in every direction. She saw Alva amble his way along the foam at the edge of surf and shore, waving his metal detector in graceful arcs in front of him like an orchestra conductor. Now and again he would stop to dig a small hole with his yellow plastic shovel and sequester the contents in one of his pockets. Avoiding the Saturday morning joggers, he carefully spread the *Finny Times* out on the dry sand and sat on it. He continued to pat his pockets as the birds stabbed nosily through his belongings. "Do you have any candy, Ruth? I'm out."

"Hi, Alva. Let me see." She began poking around in her backpack, at the same time shooing the birds away from his treasures. "I'm sorry about the birds. Did they ruin anything?"

"No way, nothing to ruin. Just a few bottle caps and a watch. Cheap Timex, no good."

Ruth victoriously held up two sticks of sugar-free gum and a mauled Snickers bar. He took the chocolate.

"Shouldn't eat that sugar-free stuff, sweet cheeks. Gives people cancer." He took out his teeth and began gumming the candy bar. "I heard about Neopolitan. Got his lights smashed out. He had it coming, I'd say."

"Why do you think someone wanted to kill Neopoli-tan, er, Napoleon?"

"I think it was mainly because he was an idiot."

She nodded.

"And the lizard."

"The what?"

"The iguana. I was picking up cans from the recycle bin behind the gallery, and I heard him and a lady having an awful row. Regarding the iguana."

"An argument? When?"

"Last week. Day before the fire."

"Who was the lady?"

"Don't know. Shades was down. She smelled real pretty, though. Flowery. It reminded me of my Aunt Noony's flower beds. Always so nice. Except when they had the big molasses flood. Stuck up the whole town, flowers and all."

Ruth tried to usher him back to the subject at hand. "It was a lady who smelled nice."

"Real nice. Flowery. Like Aunt Noony's garden."

"What did she sound like?"

"She had a soft voice, but it got louder and louder. Then it sounded like she commenced to cryin'. Now that's a real bugger of a man, makes ladies cry. Worse than Georgie Porgie." He shook his head disgustedly, white clusters of hair dancing around his face like tufts of cotton.

"But, Alva, why were they talking about lizards?"

"Don't know. She said something about she didn't want to raise no lizard no more, and he said she would jolly well raise it until he said he wanted it back. I left after that on account of I didn't want any trouble."

"Why in the world would they be talking about iguanas?"

"Can't say. Never thought much about lizards myself. Always seemed kind of standoffish to me. Maybe they make okay pets, though. They said it was a cheerful sort. Happy."

Ruth was beginning to feel like she was trapped in a Laurel and Hardy movie. "Happy iguanas?"

"Don't that just beat it?" He stood up and shooed the birds away from his remaining candy bar. "Well, thanks for the candy, sweet cheeks. See you around." He shuffled on down the beach.

She collapsed on her back in the gravelly sand. The birds clambered over to check her pockets. If Alva was to be believed, the sweet-smelling woman with the soft voice sounded an awful lot like Dimple. Arguing with Napoleon. The day before a fire wiped out his greenhouse and a week before a fuchsia wiped out his life. Arguing. About lizards?

Did I really just have a ten-minute conversation about happy iguanas? Which one of them was the crazy one, anyway?

Chocolate-chip-fudge-death-by-triglyceride brownies.

They smelled obscenely good. That was surprising considering how long it had been since Ruth baked anything other than a frozen dinner. The afternoon culinary project gave her an excuse to put off looking for the rest of Phillip's novel. She piled the squares neatly on a Chinet plate. They provided an excuse to visit Dimple, anyway. And maybe, just maybe, a few left over for Monk.

She checked on the birds huddled on the gravel in the backyard. Grumpy. She decided to fix them their treats later when the sun came out. They always perked up on sunny afternoons.

October along the coast was the best time of year. The weather was mild after the early morning fog burned away. The fruit and vegetable stands were brimming with squash, potatoes, and artichokes. There was a smell in the air of rich loamy soil—and expectation. She wished the smells and colors would touch her the way they used to. She wished anything would.

Her thoughts rambled bumpily along, reviewing the recent chapter of Phillip's story. She found herself thinking about it often, the dark-haired Benjamina Pena and the country cop. She would conjure up images of the people she knew, whom they had grown up with, trying to find the sources of Philip's inspiration. So far, the quest remained completely frustrating.

Breathing heavily, she crested the top of Finny's Nose and worked her way down a shaded side street past a dilapidated barn and a phlegmatic billy goat. The Dent household was quite lovely and not at all dilapidated. It was a large three-story house with gables over the upper-floor windows and a slate walkway. The front was luxurious, with purple bougainvillea and hydrangeas working diligently to try to squeeze out one last bloom of the season. There was Dimple's rescued fuchsia on the front porch. Ruth shuddered and rang the bell. When there was no answer, she continued on to the guest house. She knocked gently on the front door.

No answer. She tried the bell. Still no answer. She tried knocking again and just about rapped Dimple right on the nose.

"Oh, Dimple. I hope I'm not bothering you. Is this a bad time?"

The woman looked well enough. Good color, nicely brushed hair, a pretty blue dress tied at her slender waist. About the only sign of the recent trauma were dark shadows under her eyes.

"It is always a good time to greet a neighbor."

Dimple ushered her into the sitting room. The floors and wainscoting were washed pine, and sunshine flooded through the puffy flowered drapes. It was light and airy, definitely a woman's house.

"What a lovely cottage. Did you decorate it yourself?"

"My mother and I did. She loved beautiful things."

Ruth sat on a puffy loveseat while Dimple unwrapped the brownies and started filling glasses with ice.

"Are you feeling okay?" Ruth began hesitantly.

Dimple returned with two glasses of iced tea. "Yes, thank you. I am feeling well. Just a little sad. About—him."

Ruth looked at the serious face nibbling a corner of a brownie. "Dimple, I know you and Napoleon were close. It must have been a terrible shock to find him. . .like that."

She nodded, lips trembling. "We were going to get married. Later. After the gallery was more established. We didn't tell anyone, mostly because of Daddy. He wouldn't approve, and you know what his temper is like."

Ruth knew all too well. Try as she might, she just couldn't get a mental picture of Dimple as Napoleon's wife. They were more than just opposites; rather like species from two completely different planets that did not share the same galaxy.

Dimple gazed at the glass in her hands. "Love is a thing from which all pleasures flow."

"Er, yes, it is. Does." She took a sip of tea and choked. It tasted like potpourri. "Wow. What an interesting blend. What is it?"

"My own creation. Dandelions, mint, rose hips, and

ginger. It cleanses the circulatory system."

She set the glass down, fearful of any further cleansing. "What sort of man would your father choose for you?"

Dimple stared at Ruth, looking suddenly much older. "My father has hated my mother for twenty years since she ran away. He looks upon me as a reminder of her." She nibbled on her brownie. "I live out here to get away from the angry energy that envelops him. He can only contain it for a while, and then it explodes. Anger is just helplessness disguised." She looked down at the ice swirling around in her glass.

Ruth felt a trickle of fear. "Dimple, he doesn't hurt you, does he?"

"He did when I was younger. Only a few times. Then I showed him the error in hurting another living soul."

"How did you do that?"

"I left my senior project on his pillow one morning. He was impressed."

Her brain zinged. Dimple Dent? A student? She tried not to sound too incredulous. "You were working on a degree?"

Dimple smiled. "I studied at UCLA. Botany and herbology. I love plants. I even have my own secret greenhouse in the knoll." She giggled. "Nobody ever bothers me there."

UCLA? Ruth hoped her chin had not hit her chest. Dimple Dent a college student? Or any kind of student for that matter? It really was true that still waters run deep. Or maybe cloudy waters. Uh-oh. She was beginning to think in fortunes, too.

"Did you earn a degree?" she asked.

"No. I came home for spring break three years ago

and did some odd jobs at the gallery. I got to know Napoleon." Her eyes grew misty. "He was so intelligent, so refined. He made me feel like I was, well, a beautiful woman. I never felt that way before."

She shook her head slowly from side to side. "We fell in love. At least, I fell in love." She squeezed her lids tightly together. "I never went back to school." She passed a hand over her eyes. "I have to tell you something. I—I am going to—I have become—"

"I know. I know about the baby. It's Napoleon's, isn't it?"

She didn't ask how Ruth knew. Ruth reached over and patted her hand. She could not seem to think of any sage advice, any words of wisdom that would help in such a predicament. Where were those perfect Hallmark verses when you needed them?

"Somehow it will all work out, Dimple. God will make sure of it." The hypocrisy of her own words stuck in her throat. She used to believe them until her own world splintered apart.

They sat for a few moments in silence. Dimple looked so forlorn, so childlike, that Ruth could not bring herself to ask about the altercation in Napoleon's office.

"I'd better go now. I'm sure you would like to lie down."

"Thank you for coming. And for the chocolate."

"You're welcome." The sunshine felt warm upon her face as she turned down the gravel path, but inside she felt chilled. She stopped after a few paces.

"Dimple, what was your project about? The one that you put on your father's pillow?"

"It was called "Deadly Poison in Your Backyard: A Gardener's Guide to Lethal Flowers." I got an A on that paper."

Ruth turned the knob gently and closed the door.

Thank you for coming, Ms. Finchley." The office was quiet on Saturdays. Jack led her through the empty front room to his office and gestured to the seat in front of his desk. He opened a battered spiral-bound notebook. "I just have a few detail questions. You said that you moved to New York by way of California. Did you grow up in the area?"

Red folded her hands in her lap. "My mother was from Miramar actually, so I lived on the coast until I was three or so. Then we gradually made our way across the U.S. until we wound up in New York."

"You are an artist?"

"Yeah." She laughed, a toothy grin lighting her face. "In my dreams. Actually, I really want to be a painter, but the only audience that appreciates my work is me. I work for the Shaum Gallery, so I can sort of say I'm a part of the art world."

"What do you do exactly for the gallery?"

"A little bit of everything. Press releases, community outreach, arranging exhibits, stuff like that."

He nodded. "We talked the other night about Napoleon Prinn. Tell me again how you two met."

"Last year my curator decided to do an exhibit on the ocean. All seascapes using different mediums and interpretations. It was my job to arrange a traveling exhibit from the other coast. Yours."

"And you happened upon our Finny Gallery?"

Red gazed at him intently before answering. "You aren't much of an art lover, are you?"

"Not exactly. Is that relevant?"

"Well, believe it or not, your Finny Gallery has quite a good reputation for featuring innovative, quality art. It also has an awesome Web site. I did some research over the Internet and decided to give it a shot. Mr. Prinn was excited to provide a few pieces, and he even flew out himself for the exhibit opening."

"Did you strike up a friendship with him?"

"I did my job. That's what I'm paid to do. Just like you." Her green eyes narrowed, the lashes translucent against her skin.

"How did he come to purchase a sculpture from your gallery?"

"I talked him into it. He really wanted something new and dynamic to set his gallery apart. The Carmine was a logical choice. Say what you will about the guy—he knew art, and he knew a good piece when he saw it. All I had to do was work on him. Get him to swallow the price tag."

"Which was?"

"Thirty thousand dollars."

Jack took a breath. "Quite a price tag."

"Worth every penny. The piece is awesome. I arranged for it to be flown here, and I picked it up at the airport and delivered it myself."

"Have you received payment?"

"The Shaum got half when Prinn purchased. Upon delivery we were supposed to get the other fifteen grand. He agreed to pay the other half after the gallery shindig." She paused. "I guess that's going to take awhile now, isn't it?"

"I would tend to think so. What are you going to do now?"

"I'm not sure. He didn't fulfill the monetary obligation,

so I guess the Carmine goes back to the Shaum. I'll have to talk to my curator and see what he says." Red straightened her shoulders. "Are we done here? I've got some things to do."

"Sure." Jack stood behind his desk, feeling as though he knew her only slightly better than he had a half hour ago. "By the way, do your people still live in New York?"

She grabbed her denim knapsack. "Let's just cut the small talk, shall we? You already know all the facts about my life. I'm sure you've run my particulars and have it all in that notebook. If there's anything you didn't find out, you can with a phone call or two."

He eyed her freckled face closely, surprised at her reaction. She was right, of course. He knew her mother was a New York resident, as well as the fact that she attended an art school and dropped out her senior year. She had received excellent evaluations from the Shaum Gallery, and the curator trusted her implicitly. He wasn't sure why he had asked the question. He had no reason to.

"Thank you for coming in, Ms. Finchley. We would appreciate it if you could stay in town a few more days until we get some loose ends tied up."

"All right. I've got a few days of vacation coming. Might as well spend it at the beach, even though it's so ridiculously cold here." She turned at the doorway. "By the way, Detective, I thought Napoleon Prinn was a complete jerk, but killing him would be like killing the goose that lays the golden eggs, now, wouldn't it? Why would I want to do that?"

Jack had to admit he had no idea.

The next person to enter the detective's office arrived in

a cloud of Chanel No. 5. Summer Sawyer wore tight leather pants and a silk tunic, all in a sizzling shade of red. Her shoes were high, strappy, and filled with little red-painted toes.

"Hello, Ms. Sawyer. Thank you for coming," Jack began again. "I just have a few questions for you about the Napoleon Prinn murder."

She leaned back in the chair and crossed her legs. "Fire away, Detective."

"You knew Prinn through his connection to your university. He was going to show some of your students' work at the dedication of the gallery, but at the last minute he decided it wasn't up to snuff. Is that about the size of it?"

"Yes." The small silver hoops flashed against her black hair as she nodded thoughtfully. "I guess that's about it."

He looked at her for a beat or two. So much for helping the police. "And how did you take that decision?"

"Take it? I took it to be a really lousy decision. There is nothing substandard about that art. He was just bent out of shape because I criticized his choice of sculpture."

"How exactly did you criticize it?"

"I told him he paid too much for it. He really doesn't, didn't, know much about sculpture. The piece is lovely and well executed, but he would have done better with some advice from people who specialize in sculpted works."

"You, for instance?"

"I could have directed him." She clasped her hands over one knee, lacing the French-manicured fingers together.

He decided to be blunt. "How has Prinn's rejection affected your career?"

She raised an eyebrow. "Negatively. That's pretty

obvious, isn't it?"

"How negatively?"

"If you weren't so handsome, Detective, I might not find you charming. His rejection set me back in the eyes of the trustees, which will delay my plans for promotion for a while." She smiled and folded her arms. "He slowed me down, that's all. I'll get what I want in the long run. I always do."

He didn't doubt that for a second. "What do you know about Prinn's death?"

"Only that he was clobbered in his study. I was out in the gardens getting some air after the, uh, entertainment portion of the evening. The nasty scene between Wanda and Red. Did you hear about that?"

He nodded. "Go ahead and tell me your impression."

She thought for a moment. "It seemed like a good old-fashioned catfight to me, although I don't know what the cause of their animosity is. They're not in love with the same man or anything conventional like that." She laughed.

"And after your stroll?"

"We all assembled in the dining room to wait for Napoleon. March gave that ridiculous toast, and then the little fainting girl showed up."

"Do you have any idea who would want to kill Napoleon?"

"Anyone who knew him would be my guess."

"Ms. Sawyer, did you have a physical relationship with Mr. Prinn?"

She laughed, white teeth gleaming against satiny red lipstick. "No, Detective. He just isn't my type." She looked at him through lowered lashes. "I can't resist a man with a badge."

He blinked several times, trying to unfog his retinas before continuing. Jack was accustomed to interviewing old ladies with lost cats or farm laborers with property disputes. Maybe an addict here or there and occasionally a homicide or two would crop up, usually the result of drugs or jilted lovers. It had been awhile since he encountered a piranha woman.

"You have been staying at the Finny Hotel since the day before the murder. Did you meet any of the other guests?"

"Hmmm. I met the redheaded freckly girl. She kept to herself. And a middle-aged man, bald. Really nice clothes. What was his name? I think it began with a *B*."

"Buck Pinkey?"

She snapped her fingers. "That's it. He was a real smooth talker."

"What did you talk about?"

"Oh, nothing much. He bought me an iced tea. Come to think of it, he didn't say much about his business."

"That doesn't surprise me."

"Why?"

"He works for a drug cartel."

Her eyebrows went up. "Incredible. I should have had him buy me lobster, too."

"You didn't pick up on any details about his comings and goings?"

"No. He got a call on his cell phone while we noshed. He didn't talk long, just said he was going to be staying for a few more days."

"That's it?"

"Yes. I think so."

"You didn't overhear any names?"

"No. He hung up and we went our separate ways."

"Anyone else from the hotel that you. . .became acquainted with?"

"Not really," Summer said.

"Okay. I think I've got pretty much all I need. Thanks for coming down here. I'd appreciate you staying in town a few more days. I hope you're enjoying Finny."

"I'd enjoy it a lot more with some company. It's so quiet in Finny. What do you do for fun?"

Jack was not sure how to answer this one. "Well. . ." He cleared his throat as he opened the office door for her. "There's always the library."

Ruth had fallen asleep in the rocker, dreaming of man-eating flowers, when a noise startled her awake. She sat up, disoriented and unsure why she had awakened until the knock repeated itself. Glancing at the clock, she wondered who would come to call at nine forty-five on a Saturday evening, or any evening for that matter, as she padded quietly to the door and squinted through the peephole. Astonished, she let in the detective and his boy.

The child was asleep, cheeks flushed, hair tousled. He was wearing footed Batman pajamas and clutching a blanket under his chin. The detective looked sheepish.

"I am so sorry to bother you this late. I just have to ask you something. It's been driving me crazy, and I can't sleep until I get an answer. I called, but you didn't pick up. I know this is really way too late to be dropping in."

She guided him into the sitting room, and he gingerly lowered himself into a bentwood rocker without waking the child in his arms.

"Would you like some coffee?"

"No, no. Don't go to that trouble. I'm bothering you enough already."

"Forgive my forthrightness, but I am a pretty good judge of faces. Your mouth said, 'No coffee, thanks,' but your eyes said, *I would commit heinous crimes for just one cup.*"

He laughed quietly, continuing to rock the boy. "Is it that transparent? So much for my stony detective face. The coffeemaker at work is on the fritz, so I am way behind on my caffeine intake."

She vanished into the kitchen. As she brewed a pot, she thought how ridiculously pleasant it was to serve someone again. She poured the strong brew into one of the nice mugs.

He took it gingerly, holding it well away from the boy's body.

"He is darling," she said quietly. "I haven't seen him for a while." He looked exactly like his mother, she thought. "So precious."

"Thanks. I've gotta be a really bad parent to drag him out of bed, but he can sleep through a train wreck, so I was hoping it wouldn't mess up his schedule too much. Louella watches him when I'm at work. She's so great about coming over when I get a call, even in the wee hours, I just didn't want to ask any more of her today." He rubbed the boy's fleecy back in little circles. "Sometimes I think she's more of a parent to him than I am," he said.

"I think Paul knows who his daddy is. Has he shown any progress?"

He closed his eyes and sighed. "No, not really. He hasn't spoken since Lacey died. Even when he cries he does it silently. I've tried everything his therapist has recommended. I even bought him a mynah bird. Can you believe that? I thought Paul would be interested in teaching it to talk. It doesn't say a word either. Anyway, I should get to the point, Ruth, after barging in at this late hour. I came over after your near miss and we talked awhile. Why do I know the name Heston Blue? Did we discuss him?"

"Not him. It."

"Huh?"

"It. Heston Blue is a plant. The fuchsia that I, er, took from the garbage pile at the gallery, remember?"

"A plant," he repeated dully. "What is going on in this town?" He glanced down sharply to see if he had woken the child.

She waited, watching the wheels spinning in Jack's mind. His eyes darted back and forth as if he were reading a message graffitied inside his skull.

"Ruth, you are not going to believe this, but Napoleon Prinn's next of kin is a son. The name on the birth certificate is Heston Blue."

A quarter of an hour later, Ruth was trailing behind Jack as he walked back out to his car. He deposited Paul, gently strapping him into the car seat. They were both quiet for a moment, trying to put the bizarre pieces together. Could it be coincidence that a mysterious person delivered a plant to Napoleon Prinn called Heston Blue? The name of his son? And he had thrown it away, furious.

Jack said they had tracked down the woman believed to be Heston Blue's mother to Seaview Sanitarium, a mere fifty miles away; he secured permission from her doctors to interview her.

Ruth's head was whirling by the time she noticed the noise. Uh-oh. It sounded like a feathery prison break. Before she could dash to the side yard and shove the gate shut again, the inmates had made a break for it, flapping and squabbling all over the front yard.

After a moment of motionless surprise, she began running, snatching up the birds and holding their angry beaks shut while she shoved them into the backyard and slammed the gate. Grover scooted under the bushes, and Rutherford headed across the street with the speed of a fully fueled rocket, Ulysses right behind him.

"Come here, you crazy birds," she bellowed. Grover hunkered down and snapped at her hands when she tried to extricate him. She finally managed to grasp the beak and drag him from under his bunker. Flinging him in the backyard none too gently, she ran across the street for Rutherford. He was in the neighbors' herb garden, a strand of basil quivering from his beak. She returned him to the yard and joined Jack in the chase for Ulysses.

Jack finished strapping in his son before he jumped into the melee. He cornered the bird, who divided his attention between the tender grass shoots and the man attempting to capture him. Jack approached slowly, step by step, talking soothingly. "It's okay, fella. I'm not going to hurt you."

"Watch out, Jack! He has issues," Ruth hollered. Too late. She watched, hands over her mouth, as the detective grabbed Ulysses around the chest. The bird flapped furiously and paddled his yellow legs until Jack lost his grip. Not to be outdone by a bird, he careened after Ulysses as the gull galloped down the lawn and up onto the hood of his Chevy.

He pounced on Ulysses' neck, fighting off the pointy beak, panting and swiping at the blood running down from a scratch above his eye. Jack and Ulysses glared at each other, tired brown eyes staring into villainous yellow ones.

Ruth ran up to take the bird from his conqueror. "I am so sorry, Jack. How can I make it up to you?"

Jack's eyes suddenly opened wide as he turned his head to peer into the front car window.

Paul was awake, his little laugh bubbling out through the open car window and echoing down the quiet street.

Ruth had taken on the monumental task of cleaning Phillip's study while she avoided church yet again. She told herself the cleaning was long overdue, that it was a disgrace to leave it in such dishabille and it would be wrong to subject the congregation to her emerging case of sniffles.

The truth of the matter was, she was desperate to find the rest of Phillip's novel. There were so many pieces left to discover. Lately, she had only been able to locate short segments, none chronologically coherent. If she could be honest with herself, she was afraid to discover that there was no more, that she would never know where Phillip's story had taken him, would take them both.

From the file cabinet, she extracted a bulging, unlabeled file and sank with it to the floor, trying to keep the contents from sliding everywhere. It was filled with greeting cards of every variety, for every occasion. They both had been unable to throw the sentimental things away. A card he had given her on their silver anniversary brought a deep ache to the pit of her stomach. Inside on the fancy foil thing he had written, *Who would have thought we could make it from the tinfoil anniversary to the silver one? Let's go for the gold. I love you, Phillip.*

They hadn't made it to gold.

She didn't cry. There wasn't enough grief left anymore, just an overwhelming sadness.

Among the colorful collection, a brilliant red card caught her eye. It had a tremendously ugly lizard on the front wearing a plush red Santa hat. She could almost hear Phillip's voice reading the punch line inside. Iguana wish you a merry Christmas! Sheesh. So corny. So Phillip.

Snatches of the weird conversation with Alva on the beach played back in her mind. Happy lizards. Iguanas. Merry iguanas. Dimple said she didn't want to raise it anymore, and Prinn told her she would do it until he said so.

A merry iguana. Merry iguana. *Marijuana*.

It couldn't be. It was just too bizarre, too much like a funky Nancy Drew mystery. It must be a product of her depressed neuropathways.

"I even have my own secret greenhouse in the knoll," Dimple had said. *"Nobody ever bothers me there."*

It was time to bake another batch of brownies.

⸺

Ruth decided on a decoy if the brownie ploy didn't work. Herbert could use some extra attention, and there was nothing he liked more than an adventure in the countryside, a Sunday stroll to put the pep in his step. Her plan was to drop the brownies off at Dimple Dent's cottage and then take the scenic walk home.

Ruth practically had to chase Herbert until they got halfway up Finny's Nose. By then the small tern was so tired he could barely plop one bandy leg in front of the other. About a half mile before they reached the Dents' property, she hoisted him up and tucked him inside her sweat jacket with his head poking out of the top like a pop-up lawn sprinkler.

She knocked softly on Dimple's door. No answer. She knocked again louder and listened for signs of life. Nothing. She tried the bell and shouted hello.

She left the plate of brownies on the doorstep. *Well, I guess it wouldn't hurt to take a walk around the property. I don't think they have any signs posted,* she thought. She casually meandered back down the walkway, heading for the dense cluster of twisted cypress trees. As she crossed the driveway to the main house, Buster pulled up in a shower of dust.

"What are you doing here?" he asked, shoving his car keys into his pocket. He was dressed as he always was, in a faded flannel shirt and cowboy boots, a baseball cap pulled down to his bushy eyebrows.

She was suddenly furious. "What am I doing here? Are you surprised I'm still up and around after you almost ran me down?"

"You are a crackpot. And what is the matter with your stomach?"

Looking down, she realized that Herbert had rolled himself up like an armadillo when the screaming started and was quietly squawking. She looked like that scene from Sigourney Weaver's "Alien" movie right before the guy explodes.

"It's a bird. And if you can't admit what you did to me, maybe you would like to explain it to the police." She was trying to sound dignified and keep the bird still at the same time.

Buster narrowed his eyes and shoved both hands into his pockets. He grunted. "It was an accident. I didn't see you both there. I was driving too fast. I was mad about something."

Big surprise. "And you didn't think to stop and help us? Your own daughter?"

"I did stop," he said defiantly, "and you were movin' around, so I figured there was no harm done."

She shook her head in disbelief. "You almost ran down your own daughter. Doesn't that scare you at all? You could have killed her."

The red began around the flannel collar and worked its way slowly up to his neck and the stubbled chin. "I could have killed her, all right. And him, too." He smashed a fist onto the hood of the car. "I didn't raise my daughter to be like her mother. She knows better." Buster looked at her uncomfortably for a minute before examining the tops of his boots. "Never mind. That's dirty linen. Shouldn't be aired in public. Look, I am sorry for scaring you. I woulda stopped if you, either of you, was hurt." He looked suddenly old as he shuffled up the walkway, deflated, like a helium balloon on a bitterly cold day.

Before he reached the door, she called out, "What's done is done, Mr. Dent. She is still your daughter." He didn't turn back. She waited until she was sure he wasn't coming back out before she continued as surreptitiously as a person could with a bird stuffed up her clothing.

Buster was a man cruelly disappointed by life. First by his wife's betrayal, then by his daughter's liaison with a man whom he despised. Jack had told Ruth unofficially that Napoleon was killed by someone who crashed a potted plant over his head with such force that shards of the terra-cotta had been driven deep into his scalp. Prinn had to have been facing the person, so it was likely someone he knew. Someone strong, someone angry, with no regard for the sanctity of life, plant or human.

Her thoughts carried her into the woods until the path became no more than a barely discernible thread. Feeling as though she should have left a trail of bread crumbs, she worked her way gradually downward, into a tiny hollow screened by trees and dense shrubbery. She came upon it suddenly, a small greenhouse, glass paned, glinting in the sunlight pouring in through the gap in the tree line.

"I can't believe I really found it."

The huge dog that suddenly materialized at her feet began to growl, showing a very white set of pointy teeth. The growl caused Herbert to shoot up her jacket like a champagne cork and flail wildly in the vicinity of her head.

"Stop, Herbert," she hissed. "You're not supposed to move around. They can sense fear. Nice poochy. Nice doggy. I'm sure we wouldn't taste good at all. I'm old and stringy, and Herbert here would probably be pretty gamey."

The dog continued to growl, waving his head back and forth as he matched his pursuing steps to their retreating ones, saliva dripping from his jowls in frothy tendrils.

"Oh no. I think we're kibble."

"I thought I heard voices." Dimple emerged from the greenhouse and patted the slavering dog on the head. "It's okay, Pepper. This is my friend Ruth. And her friend, er—?"

"Herbert." She was too relieved to feel idiotic about introducing her bird to a vicious dog.

"Herbert. Hello, Ruth. Why don't you come in and see my greenhouse? I have never had a visitor before. The warmth of a hearth comes from the friends who sit beside it." Dimple held open the door and led them inside.

Ruth's heart gradually began to resume its duty, along with her deprived lungs. Long rectangular trays were filled with water, holding up brown pots with varying stages of plant growth. The plants closest to the wall were tiny seedlings, the ones in the center were a full five inches tall, and those bordering the walls were fully grown.

Lush, spiky, fully grown marijuana plants. Just like

those pictured on the bulletin board at the police station.

Ruth turned to face Dimple, staring at her with bulging eyes. "Dimple. Do you—? Don't you—? Hasn't anyone—?"

Dimple continued to gaze patiently.

"Do you have any idea? There are laws. You just can't— What are you growing?"

"Would you like some tea? I know you've had a shock."

"Yes. No! No, I don't want any tea. I want you to tell me about this." She gestured wildly around the greenhouse.

"Well, as you can see, the plants are all fed hydroponically. That way the nutrients are controlled and you avoid brackish water and root rot. I use a water filtration system to reduce the sulphur, which can build up in the plants if you're not careful."

Ruth stared at her.

"Of course, I am not a marijuana user myself, but I believe every plant has a right to reach its full potential. Don't you?"

This time, Ruth collected herself enough to recover her powers of speech.

"Dimple," she said quietly, only a hint of hysteria in her voice, "you do know you are growing a crop of drugs in this greenhouse?"

"Well, of course, Ruth. I'm not dense, you know. But Napoleon sold these strictly for medical use. Would you like to see my gardens outside? I have some beautiful cyclamen and a patch of lemon geranium."

"Why are you doing this? Don't you know you could be arrested? It is against the law to grow crops of marijuana! Marijuana is an illegal substance in the state of California for practically everyone!" She realized she was yelling because Herbert made another retreat into her jacket. She took a steadying breath.

Dimple's green eyes clouded in confusion. "Napoleon asked me to. He knows, he knew, I am very gifted in the nurturing of plants, so he asked me to grow some for him. He supplied the seedlings and helped me outfit the greenhouse. It goes to reputable pharmacies for research purposes. It's all legal, I'm sure."

Ruth felt as if she were in a scene from a bad movie. "What do you do when the plants are ready?"

"I dry and package them and deliver them to Napoleon. At least that's what I used to do. He sold them to research firms and doctors for treating patients. Towards the end, things became anxious, though." She lowered her eyes and continued faintly, "He would get really angry and yell if the plants weren't ready when he wanted them."

She wiped her eyes with the back of her hand. "I didn't want to grow them anymore. They just seemed to cause tension, and I wanted to plant something more inspiring. I thought perhaps peonies. Have you ever grown peonies?"

Intent on avoiding another conversation derailment, Ruth said quickly, "You must know that this is not the best thing for you."

She looked sad. "Ruth, I am not a stupid woman. Not completely, anyway. My IQ approaches the genius level, actually. I loved him, and when I did well, when it was a really good crop, he was happy with me. I believed him. About everything." The words tumbled out, like birds fledging from their nest. "He loved me. He was going to marry me." Her voice trailed away.

Ruth took her hand gently, feeling her grief, brittle as glass, wishing desperately she had some comfort to give the girl. "It's okay. I understand."

Silently, she said a prayer that Detective Denny would, too.

Napoleon Prinn was cremated, reduced to ashes like his greenhouse.

March orchestrated the memorial service at the gallery gardens. Monday was, miraculously, a warm day, almost balmy, and the white chairs stood out sharply against the deep green of the lawns and shrubbery. A glossy portrait of the gallery owner was displayed on an easel, and baskets of fantastically colored hydrangeas were scattered around.

The town had turned out in force. Maude and Flo perused the program. Flo already had a handkerchief handy to cry for the man she hardly knew. She fluttered it in Ruth's direction.

Wanda steered Bun's wheelchair off to the side of the second row of chairs and sat down next to her, arms crossed over her shantung-silked bosom. Her mouth was set in a grim line, eyes focused straight ahead. Bun shot frequent worried glances at her daughter as if she were sitting next to a vibrating hive of hornets.

Dimple sat in the front row, next to Monk and Randy. Ruth arrived a few minutes behind Red, who looked warm in her gabardine skirt and jacket. The guests seemed anxious to seat themselves quickly, avoiding social give-and-take.

Alva had taken the time to iron his overalls and squash a brown derby of questionable heritage over his grizzled head. He parked himself next to the table of cold cuts and finger sandwiches and eyed the spread carefully. Jack stood inconspicuously under the overhang, eyeing

Summer as she glided in on three-inch heels and sat gracefully in the back.

Luis Puzan hastily moved over to offer her a seat next to him.

March had called upon Henny Novato, pastor of the First United Methodist Church, to deliver the eulogy. Pastor Novato was in his seventies, a plump, ruddy-looking man who resembled a well-dressed Tweedledee.

"And in his drive to create something beautiful and lasting, Mr. Prinn worked tirelessly to improve and strengthen the bond between Finny and the larger world of art." He then asked if anyone had anything to share about the dearly beloved.

No one did.

Eventually, the group adjourned to sample the buffet. Ruth noted that the unappetizing spread was most definitely not Monk's work.

"The yellow stuff is deviled egg, and the brown stuff is some hammy sort of thing," Alva announced to the group milling around the table as he poked suspiciously at the molded salad. "Don't know about that stuff. Looks like snot." March took hold of Alva's elbow and steered him away from the food table.

"That was a nice service," Monk said to Randy, who was standing near Red and the pastor. "I'm real sorry about your brother."

"Thank you. I'm still sort of in shock about the whole thing. I never thought I wouldn't have Boney around. Even though we hated each other most of our lives, it just seems strange not to have him in my life."

Red edged next to Randy, her plate full of crackers and salami. She cleared her throat nervously, "Yeah, me, too. I'm sorry about your brother. He had a great eye for art."

Unfortunately, Wanda was just then walking by.

"A great eye? Maybe he just had a great eye for the ladies. Maybe he was buying more than art from you." Wanda elbowed past the pastor and leaned into Red's face. Her hair was wound on top of her head in an elaborate chignon, and she bobbed slightly from side to side like a dashboard hula dancer. "Why are you here, anyway? What are you to Napoleon?"

"I represent the gallery he was working with in New York," Red snapped. "I think they call it paying your respects. Isn't that why you're here?"

"What respects? He didn't respect me enough to give my work the place it deserved." She gestured wildly toward the gallery and shifted her weight quickly to prevent herself from toppling. "And you had better not say one single word about my work." Her cheeks burned an unhealthy red against her normally sallow skin.

The level of conversation had now become so loud that it had captured the attention of the entire gathering. Ruth helped Bun clear a path toward her enraged daughter, Summer clicking along behind them.

"She'll blow. She's been drinking," Bun whispered to Ruth as they dodged chairs on their way to the buffet table.

"I wouldn't dream of bad-mouthing your work, Wanda." Red smiled slowly. "I wouldn't talk about something I've never seen before. When do you think you'll start painting something besides your signature?"

Wanda stood motionless for a moment like a building before it is demolished. Slowly, she balled her hands into fists, trembling with rage.

"Hold your temper," Bun hissed.

"Now, ladies," Henny Novato began, "I really don't think this is the place for—"

Wanda launched herself at Red, knocking Henny into the buffet table and taking out the nearest row of white chairs. Ruth quickly rolled Bun a safe distance from the melee. The old lady covered her mouth with her hands.

The two women rolled around, fingers entwined in each other's hair, screaming. The onlookers dodged here and there, toppling chairs in their efforts to stay out of the way of the rolling women. A flying plate landed on the exact center of Summer's cashmere sweater, and her arms flew up into the air reflexively as if she had been shot.

Alva carefully carried his plate to a chair directly in front of the fracas and sat down to watch.

Jack emerged from the wings, grabbed a handful of Red's copper hair, and held her still, while Monk seized Wanda by the ankles. Both women stopped struggling and released their holds.

Pastor Henny knelt next to the women, deviled egg sandwich in his hair. "Ladies, let us take a moment to—"

Wanda took that moment to kick viciously, catching Monk by surprise and knocking him backward into the pastor. They both crashed into the chair immediately next to Alva, who was eating cheese sticks and nodding.

"Yep. Always gotta look out for the southern end," Alva said.

All Ruth could think to do was pat Bun on the shoulder. "Oh no. This is terrible."

Bun did not answer. She sat in wide-eyed horror.

The women were back on top of each other with Jack and Monk in pursuit once again.

"I will kill you!" Wanda screamed, eyes dilated.

From underneath the pile Red grunted, "You couldn't

come close, you stupid cow."

Jack hauled Red to her feet, and Monk did the same to Wanda. "Take Wanda to the parking lot so she can calm down. I'll call someone to take her home. I'll make sure Red stays here until things cool off."

Ruth handed Bun over to Maude, who rolled her away toward her daughter. She noticed Summer, who was peeling the plate covered with mustard off her black sweater, which left her looking like the hind end of a giant bumblebee.

"Are you all right?" she asked.

The woman's mouth hung open, and her eyes were wide in disbelief. "This is a cashmere sweater!" she screamed. Then much to Ruth's surprise, she started to cry, tears streaming down her flawless skin.

"Well, maybe we can get it off. Do you use club soda on cashmere?"

Summer looked at her as if she had suggested trying sulfuric acid. The tears were carrying trickles of mascara down her cheeks. "This is a nightmare."

Ruth led her away from the group to a quiet bench and sat down with her.

"This whole thing has been an absolute nightmare."

"What thing, Summer?" Ruth asked gently.

"Everything was going so well. Do you know I am the youngest person to be a dean at Pomponio? Not to mention, a female dean. That's even more incredible. Don't you think so?" She turned her watery gaze on Ruth.

"Yes. That is something to be proud of. I'm sure your parents are delighted."

"Sure. Delighted. Mom anyway. It doesn't compare to being a doctor to the teeming masses, but it wasn't bad for a girl who got herself kicked out of two high schools. That stupid jerk had to ruin my chances for the chancellor's appointment, just because I wounded his pride by telling him he paid too much for his sculpture. The old geezers at the university weren't exactly jumping at the chance to appoint a young woman anyway, but I brought so much positive attention and funding to the art department, they were really going to do it, until Napoleon bent their ears, that is."

"Will they consider you again in the future?"

"I doubt it. Universities don't like scandals. I may have to go elsewhere to get another chance." Summer reached into her tiny purse and extracted a compact. Snapping it open, she examined her face. "I must look terrible."

Ruth watched her powder and plump up her face and thought it must be a burden to be beautiful; it required such a lot of maintenance. She had never been bothered by it, so time's merciless march across her eyelids and under her chin did not cause her undue trauma. The gorgeous ones must have such a difficult time watching the tiny changes that creep in from year to year.

"Listen, I don't know why I'm blabbing all of this stuff to you. I guess you just have one of those nice listening faces."

Summer got up, smoothing her skirt. "I suppose I'd better go find another sweater." She walked a few paces before adding, "Um, thanks for, you know, listening."

Ruth returned to the garden to find the remaining guests attempting to repair the damage. Nathan was just driving away, Bun and Wanda in the backseat of his car. The pathetic sight of the ruined service deepened her own growing gloom. The buffet lay squashed and trampled in the grass. Dimple retrieved Napoleon's portrait from the muddy ground, looking sadly at a big hole where his left eye should have been. She was trying to wipe away some of the grime with a pink Kleenex.

The unfortunate Pastor Novato was sitting down with his fingers pinching the bridge of his nose to staunch the flow of blood.

"I'm so sorry, Pastor. I never dreamed in a million years it would turn into a brawl," March lamented, handing him another Kleenex.

"Are you holding up okay?" Ruth asked Randy as he wandered around righting overturned chairs. Randy didn't answer.

Alva remained in his chair in the middle of the devastation, licking deviled egg from his fingers. "Yup," he said, nodding, "never bet against a redhead."

Ruth sprawled on the sofa in the afternoon sun, recalling bits and pieces from the morning's disastrous memorial service. The pastor covered in deviled egg, two women flailing at each other for all they were worth, and Napoleon's portrait with its painted eye stomped out.

It was sad, really, Ruth thought as she brewed a cup of Earl Grey. All those people at his memorial service and none of them cared for Napoleon except Dimple, a woman who had been used and exploited, left in disgrace to have Prinn's baby. Maybe Randy held on to some feelings from childhood, though he seemed more lost than grieved. The whole situation was just bizarre. It would make a great television drama.

Ruth settled on the sofa on her favorite end trying not to listen to the ticking of the grandfather clock. Opening the tattered red folder, she began to read.

The lighting was soft, like the music, wrapping around the linen-covered tables and glinting off the brass quartet in the corner. Roper looked out of place in his uniform, camped behind the beverage table as inconspicuously as a six-foot-four, two-hundred-pound man can be in a ballroom.

She walked in. He stopped breathing along with several other men in the vicinity. Her hair was twisted into a loose pile on her head, a few long black tendrils floating around her face. The dress was long, backless. It was green, the perfect shade.

Catching sight of him, she walked over to the beverage table.

"Hi, Rope." She looked anxious. "Is my dress zipped in the back?" she whispered to him. "Everyone is staring. Is my skirt tucked into my underwear or something?" Casually, she turned her back to him, pretending to scan the room.

He squelched a grin. "No, ma'am. Everything is zipped and tucked properly."

"Hmmm. Then why is everyone staring at me?"

He cleared his throat. "I think, Ms. Pena, it's because you are the most beautiful woman they've ever seen. At least, that's why I'm staring."

She looked at him for a minute. Then she laughed. "You have that Southern charm thing down to a science. Why don't you just dance with me, you nut?"

"I would love to, ma'am, but I'm on duty." The university had been receiving bomb threats with more and more frequency in the last semester, causing the evacuation of the campus on two separate occasions.

"No dancing on duty, huh? Okay. I can accept that, but you really need to call me Benjamina. I mean, we've been out on a date, haven't we? Doesn't that count for something?"

It counted for a truckload, at least for him. He wasn't sure it had been quite so meaningful for her. He was trying to get up the courage to ask her out for a second time when John Toulouse, the district attorney, put his hand on her shoulder.

"Hello, Ms. Pena. It is such a pleasure to see you again. You look absolutely beautiful, as usual. Come with me so I can introduce you to some people." He steered her away. She tried to twist out of his grasp.

"Actually, I was talking to Officer Mackey."

"I'm sure you'll see him again in the parking lot. You are

babysitting cars tonight, aren't you, Mackey?" He laughed as he led her away, a flash of perfectly capped white teeth.

"Troglodyte," Roper muttered under his breath.

━━━

It was almost eleven when Roper finished his umpteenth round of checking the parking lot. The only critters up to no good were the rats foraging around the Dumpster. He climbed back up the sixteen steps to the foyer and leaned against the wall, waiting to begin the umpteenth-and-one check of the lot. What a way to spend a shift.

He heard the whisper of silk before he heard the sniffling. He could only make out her silhouette in the moonlight, but he recognized the perfume. She was bent over, her forehead resting against the handrail. He cleared his throat gently to avoid scaring her.

She leaped upright, hands clutched together over her chest. "Oh, Roper. You scared me!"

"I'm very sorry about that. Are you. . .all right?" He could see the glint of tears in her eyes, her chest heaving rapidly.

Her voice shook slightly. "I—yes. I'm fine."

Another voice behind them startled them both. It was Toulouse.

"Well, here you are. I was wondering where you'd gotten to." He took a step toward her with an outstretched hand, and she jerked backward, directly into Roper's unyielding front.

"Your bracelet." The gold bangle glittered between his fingers in the moonlight. "It must have come unfastened while we talked. Why don't you come back inside and I'll help you put it on?"

Roper could feel her tight against him, trembling. "No. I—need some air."

"Wonderful idea. Let's go for a walk, shall we?"

"No. I want to talk to Rope, to Officer Mackey."

"Surely you don't want to miss out on that amazing brass group?"

"I'll be there in a minute."

The attorney's eyes narrowed slightly. "All right. I'll be looking for you inside shortly, then." He turned on his heel and strode back toward the soft strains of trumpet and trombone.

She waited until the door closed silently before she turned to face Roper.

"I want to go home. I'm not feeling well. Could you call me a cab? Please?"

"I'll do better than that. I'll take you home myself." He spoke quietly into the radio on his shoulder.

"I don't want you to get in trouble."

"Don't worry about that. My partner can cover the next few rounds."

Two minutes later he was walking her to the car, sandwiching her among the radio and computer console. The only noise was the static from the radio and the calm, intermittent voice of the dispatcher.

He wasn't sure what to do. Something had upset her, but she didn't want to talk about it, and he wasn't sure he should push. He walked her to her door and unlocked it.

"Thank you for driving me home. It was really kind of you." She smiled wanly. "I guess it's better riding in the front of a cop car than the back."

"I suppose so. Are you sure you don't want to talk about it?"

Suddenly she wrapped her arms around his neck, pressing her face into the bare skin under his chin. "I wish you could stay here with me," she said in a voice so muffled *by uniform that he almost didn't hear her.*

Gently, he raised her chin to look into her face. "Why don't you tell me what happened? Did someone bother you? Was it Toulouse?" His face hardened as he spoke the name.

"No. No one. I think I'm just catching something." She tried to smile brightly.

He looked unconvinced. "I'm off at one. I'm going to come by and check on you."

"I'll be asleep."

"I'll call you from my car."

"I'll be asleep. I won't hear the phone ring."

"Then you'll hear me break down the front door."

She stared at him. "I'll answer the phone."

"Good." He brushed the hair out of her eyes and leaned down to kiss her forehead.

"Thank you."

He reluctantly let her go. "Good night, Benjamina."

Ruth put the folder down and sighed. Benjamina should just level with the cop; he seemed like a good man who adored her. How often does a girl run into that sort of thing? What was the problem? Was it a skeleton from the past flying out of her closet or just a case of modern-day woman trying to juggle more than one man? And why was this novel consuming all her energy? Angrily, she began flipping through the folder, trying to find the next section in the mish-mash of papers, when the phone rang.

"Hello?"

"It's Ellen, at the library."

As if there could be another Ellen Foots lurking

somewhere other than the library. "Oh, hi. What can I do for you?"

"You could return your library books on time. You have a copy of *Fuchsias: A Plant for All Seasons*. It was due back yesterday. There is a ten-cent-per-day fine, you know."

She had completely forgotten about the book. It was sitting on the coffee table buried under a pile of catalogues. She hadn't even opened it.

"Oh brother. I forgot all about it. I'll bring it in today. I promise."

"That would be helpful. Mr. Donnelly returned it on time. I was surprised; he didn't seem like the type that would respect library rules particularly, but I guess you can't judge a book by its cover." She laughed at her joke.

Ruth rolled her eyes upward. *Just what this town of Finny needs: murder, mayhem, and a comic Nazi librarian.*

"Thanks for the call. I'm sorry to have forgotten."

"Remember the library closes at 4:00 on Mondays, so finish your book and get it back here before we lock up."

"Sure thing, Ellen." Ruth hung up and rummaged through the stack on the table. Plopping down on the sofa, she flipped through the beginning chapters.

There were many glossy pictures and all sorts of advice for growing fuchsias using salt-free cocoa fiber, plant hormones, and antioxidants. She wondered how the things ever managed in the wild, as she figured they must have at one time or another.

She was about to close the book when she noticed that the bottom right-hand corner of a page had been dog-eared and then folded flat again. It was a photo of a lush, bushy fuchsia covered with gaudy orange and purple paper lantern blossoms. The common name printed in italics was *Payoff*.

Hmmm. She began going page by page, searching for telltale creases. There were only two other pages in the entire three-hundred-page volume that had been folded. One photo showed a plant completely covered with tiny blue flowers, common name *Mary Jane*.

Mary Jane. Tiny blue blossoms. "*This particular variety can have red or blue blooms.*" Ruth smacked a hand to her forehead. "That's the plant Dimple was holding outside the gallery. The plant Napoleon had told her to take."

Frantically, she looked at the remaining page. White flowers edged in pink. The same plant she had in her kitchen, the one she had rescued from the gallery compost pile. The same variety she watched Prinn heave out the greenhouse door in a fit of rage. A Heston Blue.

The name of Napoleon Prinn's son.

March yelped as she opened her office door to find a detective seated on the settee. "You scared me."

"Sorry," Jack said.

"Don't you people ever call before you barge on in?" Her face shifted from shocked to annoyed. "I have a million things to take care of. Is there something in particular you want?"

"I'd like to know what you want."

"What?"

"What do you want, March? What are you looking to get out of this life?"

"You've got to be kidding me. This sounds like a talk show. What does it matter what I want?"

"I know what your parents wanted for you."

She started and then looked away, taking off her wool blazer and hanging it on the hook behind the door. "What do you know about my parents?"

"I know they raised two kids. They both worked two jobs to send you to college, but it wasn't enough to cover it."

"So?" Her eyes were hard, narrowed.

"So your dad took out a second mortgage on the house."

"Uh-huh. Lots of people do that, Detective. What does that have to do with the price of eggs in China?"

He paused for a moment and looked into her eyes. "He has a balloon payment due by the end of the year, and it looks like he's going to lose the house."

She was swallowing convulsively now. "Yes. Well. He invested a lot of money in my career, and it looks like my life's work is going up in smoke. I guess you know all about me, don't you?" Her voice rose with every word. "I'll tell you what, Detective, you don't know anything about me."

He waited a moment before answering quietly, "I know your parents had a son."

March spat, "My brother? So you know all about my brother, huh? Then I guess you know he's dead. I guess you know that Chili was supposed to pick me up at school. Charles was his name, but we all called him Chili. I was sixteen and waiting for him to pick me up, but he forgot. I stood on the school steps for an hour until the gym teacher gave me a ride.

"I was furious when I got home, furious at being embarrassed in front of my friends. I let him have it, all right, and my parents agreed with me. They said he was grounded for the weekend. All of a sudden he was furious, too, shouting at me for getting him grounded." She glared at the detective. "I guess you know what I said to him? No? I told him I wished I didn't have a brother. Well, he got in his car and forty-five minutes later I didn't."

Tears were streaming down her face, her mascara running into shadowy pools under her eyes. "Do you know what that's like, Detective? To always regret the idiotic last words you said to someone?"

"Actually, I do. The last words I said to my wife were 'Don't forget to pick up my uniform at the dry cleaners.' She died before my shift was over."

The silence dragged on as she stared at him. He could see the anger melting away, leaving undiluted grief in its wake.

"I am sorry. I really am." She wiped a Kleenex under her eyes and blew her nose. "How do you live with it?

Does it ever go away?"

"No. I just try to remember the nice things I said to her when I wasn't being a moron."

"Why did you come here to talk about my family? What does my father's financial trouble have to do with anything that's happened?"

"Because I think you had a plan to bail him out. A plan that involved this gallery and the keys you took from Napoleon's study the night he was murdered."

Her face was white and rigid. She opened her mouth, but nothing came out.

"Let me tell you what I think. I think that you took the keys from Prinn's office. I think you used them to unlock the file cabinet that had the safe access codes, which he changed weekly. I think you were going to remove a sum of money from the safe and get out of Dodge. How am I doing?"

"How do you know these things?" she whispered.

"Only two sets of fingerprints on the keys, yours and his." He was fudging here. The crab bisque pretty much rendered the prints inconclusive. "You mentioned he had come into some money recently." He paused before adding, "You purchased two plane tickets on a red eye to Seattle for the night of the dedication. The folks are from Seattle, aren't they?"

He leaned forward. "Look, Ms. Browning. I have spent a lifetime dealing with bad people. Crooks, dealers, extortionists, murderers, pedophiles, you name it. I know bad people. You are not bad people."

She looked up at him, desperation spilling from every pore. "Napoleon had all these grand plans for this place. A total renovation, traveling exhibits, maybe even opening up a sister gallery on the East Coast. I was totally caught up in it, of course. I thought we were going to make it big after all these years." She shook her head. "I mean, it was really the chance of a lifetime. A chance to get in on the ground floor, to build a gallery from the bottom up. Who could pass that up?

"Anyway, we were really starting to get some acclaim, features in regional papers and even some notice from the big boys back East. Napoleon decided to begin the renovation of the building and buy a few significant pieces from the Shaum.

"Last December, I began to notice that something was wrong; Napoleon was acting strangely, getting weird phone calls, disappearing for periods of time. He would show up at the beginning of each month with a satchel that went immediately into the safe. I knew it was money, but I didn't know it was from drugs. I thought he was gambling or borrowing from loan sharks or something."

She began gnawing on a fingernail that was already bitten to the quick.

"Was it your idea? To take the money?"

"No. Well, I can't say I hadn't thought of it. Napoleon treated me like a farmhand. Oh, I know he probably hired me because I don't look bad in a skirt and I played the pretty office girl to the public. But I got all the menial jobs and he cut me out of the good stuff, the buying and marketing decisions, I mean."

He steered her back to the topic, which was on the top of his list. "He deserved to get taken. Is that what Randy said?"

She removed the bitten fingernail and started on another. "I told Randy about the money that Napoleon put in the safe on the first of every month. I knew it was a lot, maybe thousands. It would definitely be something to help my parents and enough maybe for Randy to start a theater. I told him that Napoleon was into something shady and I wanted out before I got taken down along with him. We worked out the plan together."

"Go on."

"My part was to get the keys from his office and find the safe codes. We would wait until the dedication was over and things were locked up for the night. I have a key to the building and the alarm codes, so getting in wouldn't be a problem. We were going to come back, take the money, and then get to the airport."

"How did the keys wind up in Ruth Budge's soup?"

She blushed. "I can't believe it, but I dropped them in Monk's soup pot."

"How?"

"I took the keys from the office, and I was going to open the filing cabinet when I heard some people coming. I didn't have time to replace them, so I went out the back door and walked around to the dining room. My dress didn't have any pockets, and when I snuck through the French doors to join the dinner, Monk swooped down on me demanding that I give the toast. He wanted to get the dinner served before it was ruined, I guess. I panicked and the keys slipped from my hand into the bisque before he reached me."

Jack smiled, picturing the enraged navy officer bellowing about his crab chowder or whatever it was. "You said you heard voices, people coming into Prinn's office. Could you recognize the voices?"

"No. One could have been a woman's; I'm not sure."

"Did they sound angry?"

"Not that I could tell." She took a breath and stared

at him. "Detective, are you going to arrest me? Us?"

He returned her gaze. "At the present time, it doesn't appear that you and Randy actually committed any crimes. Lucky for you, your plans were derailed."

"Yeah," she breathed, relieved, "but not so lucky for Napoleon."

30

Ruth caught up with March in Napoleon's office, shortly after Jack drove out of the parking lot. He waved cheerfully at her, but she could see that he looked tired. The secretary was talking on the phone and gestured for Ruth to sit down. Since the gallery was officially closed, she was dressed casually in jeans and a lily pad–green sweater.

Ruth avoided the discolored splotches on the carpet and made her way to a chair in the corner, under the coatrack.

"All right. Thank you." She slammed the phone down.

"Never mind there's been a murder here and our gallery is closed down. This guy just has to have that painting to go over his sofa. I don't know why I feel compelled to stay on and sort this mess out. Let's go to my office. This place gives me the creeps."

They settled in next door.

"What can I do for you? Please don't tell me you bought a painting from us recently."

"No, no. Nothing like that. I wanted to ask you about a plant."

She looked amused. "A plant?"

"Yes. The plant that was used to kill Napoleon."

March closed her eyes and sighed gustily. "I've already been through this with the police! But I guess I could stand a few more questions."

"Where did it come from? The plant, I mean."

"I don't know. It just sort of appeared in his office

right before the dedication. He seemed really ticked about it. He grilled me about where it came from, who delivered it, et cetera. The fact of the matter is, I don't have a clue. He asked me to get rid of it, but I didn't have time before the ceremony started."

"What did it look like?"

"You saw it, didn't you?"

"Yes," Ruth said slowly, "but I was sort of, distracted, by what was underneath it."

March nodded, crinkling up her nose. "Yes, well, I'm not much of a plant person, but I know it was a fuchsia. Lots of green leaves, white flowers with pink edges."

"Payoff."

"What?"

"Oh, nothing. I was just thinking aloud. Thanks for your help. I'll let you get back to your job."

She laughed bitterly. "Some job. See you later, Ruth."

Outside, Ruth sat down on a wrought iron bench, her head whirling.

"This has got to be more than a coincidence." Napoleon had at least four fuchsias delivered to him by a mystery person. She had one in her kitchen. Dimple had another. One got smashed to bits on the sidewalk outside the greenhouse, and the fourth killed Napoleon at the gallery soiree. The Heston Blues, a Mary Jane, and a Payoff. Presumably Donnelly had caught on to this. What did it mean?

Was someone delivering messages to Napoleon in plant language? What was the message?

The Mary Jane must refer to the marijuana that

Prinn was busily smuggling out sandwiched in paintings. Someone must have found out and began blackmailing him, hence the Payoff. Heston Blue?

She sat upright, remembering a whispered conversation in the library. "*I knew someone who was involved with a plant freak—even named a child after one.*"

She set off for the Zimmerman house.

Ruth rang the doorbell twice before she heard the humming of a motor approaching the front door.

"Who is it?" rasped a voice.

"It's Ruth Budge."

The door opened and Bun peeked out, looking surprised. She was dressed in a paisley smock and orthopedic sandals, her hair oozing out of its braid like smoke.

"Wanda is out now. She went to talk to some other galleries in San Gregorio. Won't be back until late."

Ruth breathed a silent prayer of thanks. "Actually, I need to talk to you."

The old woman blinked watery eyes. "Oh. Well, okay. Could you go around back and meet me there? The place is a mess. There's a gazebo out there. I'll bring tea or something."

She picked her way to the gate and threw her entire body weight against it to force it open. The yard was overgrown, tall brown grass bent gracefully over the slate walkway.

She walked to the rickety gazebo. Looking around the dingy yard, she noticed a white terrier sitting in a doggy igloo watching her. He was so intense, so still.

Bun's voice in her ear startled her. "He's stuffed. Name was Poppet. Wanda loved him like a child, goofy old thing." Ruth wasn't sure if she was describing the dog or the owner.

"He was her whole life after that boozing bum of a husband left her. She was much better off with just the dog." Bun considered the stuffed creature. "Broke her heart when he died, though. She cried for months. You wouldn't believe it, but she still comes out here every night and talks to him. Covers him up with a blanket if it's cold."

She slowly followed Bun up the ramp to the gazebo. The thought of a grown woman, a woman who seemed confident to a fault, sitting outside in the rain seeking comfort from a stuffed dog was pitiful. It made her own life look positively cheerful.

Bun rolled up the ramp to the gazebo, a tray with two sodas and a box of Fig Newtons balanced on her lap.

She waited while Bun slowly tore the box of cookies open, pinching the carton between her left elbow and side and ripping it open with her right hand. Ruth opened the sodas and they sipped for a minute.

"I was remembering a conversation we had at the library earlier. Something you said stuck in my mind, and I wanted to ask you about it."

Bun regarded her under bushy brows and over the rim of her soda can. "So ask."

She took a deep breath. "I was looking at a book about fuchsias. You said that you knew someone who named their child after a plant. I'd like to hear more about that."

"Why?"

"Call me curious, Bun. I'd really like to know."

"It was a long time ago."

"When you were a nurse?" She corrected hastily, "When you worked for the hospital?"

"Mmm-hmm. I did a lot of home care in those days. For people who couldn't afford the hospital trip or just didn't trust organized health care. Nobody makes house calls anymore."

"That's true. So this was a patient of yours? The one who liked plants?"

"Oh, she didn't like plants. It was the boyfriend, if you could call him that. She was totally infatuated with him. He was a sharp one, smooth. Told her what she wanted to hear to get what he wanted."

"What was that?"

Bun gave her a look.

"Oh," Ruth said, blushing, "that."

"Yeah, that. Jenny was a real looker. Gorgeous, but pathetic. She wanted that man to marry her, and she'd have done just about anything to get him."

"He wasn't interested? In the marriage thing, I mean?"

"No. She wasn't his type, no wealthy family connections, no social ambition." Bun leaned back in her chair, her eyes distant and pained. "She was just a real sweet girl. A sweet, misguided girl."

"Please tell me what happened. I really need to know."

"Same thing that always happens: She got pregnant. I was there at the birth. He wasn't, of course. He dumped her early on, even before she knew she was expecting. Why can't these girls wait for the marriage license like the good Lord intended?

"She wrote to him, begged him to come back. Said she wanted them to be a family, said the child needed a father. Told him she named the kid after one of his plants. Can you imagine? Naming a child after a plant? Heston something or other. I had to ask twice to get it right on the birth certificate."

"The man was Napoleon Prinn, wasn't he?"

She looked at Ruth with ill-concealed disgust. "Yes."

"And the woman?"

"I don't see how that pertains." Her words were slurred.

"Please, Bun."

The woman watched her for a long moment. "All right. I guess it's all water under the bridge now. Jenny Tibbets. She's in a mental hospital now. After he abandoned her, she sort of lost her mind. She kept it together for a while, for the child. Then she packed up and moved somewhere. I lost track of both of them."

"How long ago was that?"

"Twenty-three, twenty-four years ago, maybe."

"Did you know the boy well?"

"Not at all. I was there at the birth and a few times afterwards. That's all. Why are you so interested in all this, Ruth?"

"I think Heston Blue was blackmailing Napoleon before he was killed."

"The gossip is that it was a stranger. Got in and killed him for the money in the safe."

"I don't think so."

"You should stay out of it, Ruth. It's for the police to solve."

"I just stumbled across some things."

"Well, don't you pay any mind to it. I know it wasn't Heston. He's long gone."

"How do you know? Would you even recognize the

man if he was here in Finny?"

"Just leave it alone." Bun leaned forward, eyes intense. "It's not your business."

Ruth felt a twinge of fear. "Maybe you're right. Thanks for your time." She brushed Fig Newton crumbs off her lap as she rose.

Bun reached over the peeling table to return the cans and cookie box to the tray. As she did so, Ruth got a glimpse of her right hand. The fingers were strong, muscular, stained with smears of green and rust-colored paint. They both looked up and stared at each other for a long moment.

"It's you," Ruth whispered before she had a chance to think better of it. "Why do you let her take credit for your work?"

The old woman was silent for a moment. "All I need is to paint. Wanda needs to be famous. We don't always wind up with the talent that goes along with our dream. It's nobody's business but ours. You see?"

Ruth nodded. It was not her place to judge this strange symbiosis between mother and daughter. "I see. Thank you, Bun."

31

The sun finally burned its way through the fog that hugged Finny's Nose, leaving only a wispy mustache of white behind. Exactly five days after Napoleon Prinn's murder, Jack stood squinting perplexedly in the sunlight at the front door of Dimple Dent's house. He rang the doorbell.

Ruth opened the door. "Hi, Jack. Thanks for meeting me here. I know it seems weird, but I need to show you a few things." She tried to organize all the details that emerged from her meeting with Bun.

He scanned the room quickly before plopping in an overstuffed paisley chair with his back to the wall. Cop habit. Dimple was nowhere.

"So how have you been? How is Paul?"

"We've both been fine, Ruth, and you?"

"I've been fine. I mean, things have been strange lately, but really, when you consider all the things that could—"

He waited patiently until she ran out of words. "You have got my undivided attention for the time being. I assume these 'things' you need to discuss involve Dimple?"

"First of all, I need to tell you some wild theories that I've been cooking up about Napoleon's murder. It may concern Crew's, too." She began her elaborate story, starting from her library book discovery and ending with her theory that Heston Blue was a killer. "I think it couldn't be a coincidence that Donnelly was researching the same exact plants that were being delivered mysteriously to Napoleon."

Jack's eyes had gotten progressively wider.

She related her conversation with Bun, omitting the detail about the painting. "So you see, Bun nursed Heston Blue's mother, it seems, the woman you found in the sanitarium."

It was very quiet in the cottage when she finished, the only sound coming from the occasional *kerplunk* of the ice maker in the kitchen.

"Ruth, I have got to say you are the most efficient busybody I have ever met in my life."

She looked down, chewing on her bottom lip.

"And I am totally impressed. We've been looking for this Heston Blue since the night Ulysses wiped me out in your front yard, and we've gotten zip. The guy was a phantom. No marriage certificate, no DMV record or credit history, not even a voter registration. I have to say, though, we never even came close to the fuchsia clues. I didn't even know a fuchsia was a plant until you told me." He shook his head.

"Napoleon was a bad boy before he was killed," Jack continued. "He was smuggling drugs for the Mexican cartel, and Donnelly's murder put him off schedule. The cartel does not like to be put off schedule. We think one of their guys torched the greenhouse as a warning. We have a warrant out for the man you know as Buck Pinkey, but so far, he's smoke. Forgive the pun."

"Well then, maybe it was the cartel that killed Prinn?" For some reason, Ruth did not want Napoleon's son to have murdered his own father.

"Too messy. They don't generally do the murder-by-plant thing. Profit is their number one priority, and they figured out it's easier to grow the stuff in the States than trying to smuggle it across the border. That's why we started taking a look around for the plant boy, Napoleon's next of kin."

"Did you talk to Heston's mother?"

He nodded. "Yes. She wasn't much help, though. She's pretty out there. Mostly she just sang songs and brushed her hair when we talked to her. The staff has never heard her mention a son, and she's never had a visitor that they know of. Oh. Here's something an aid found in an old book on her shelf."

He handed her a copy of a worn photo. It was a black-and-white, though the colors had faded enough that everything was a darker or lighter patch of gray. A baby, propped up on fat little hands and tummy, peered out from the picture; a knit cap obscured the hair, and two tiny teeth poked out from a gummy, wet grin.

"Heston Blue?"

"Hard to say. It was the only photo they found."

She peered into the picture, mesmerized by the thought that this small innocent had grown up to be a killer. "Poor woman. Maybe it's a blessing she has checked out of the real world. Could I get a copy of this?"

"Keep that one. It's scanned. We have the original."

She stood up and moved uneasily to the window, looking out on the lush lawn and pots of flowers. "What about the keys? In the bisque? Do you think it was another message from Heston before he killed Napoleon?"

"No. I think we've got the key thing straightened out. It was a misunderstanding." He folded his arms across his flannel shirt. "Okay. Now tell me the part I don't want to hear," he said.

She looked up guiltily. "Huh?"

"The part that concerns Dimple, the part that you're scared to tell me. Let me have it, Ruth."

"I think we'd better talk on the way."

He threw out a hand and sighed. "Onward, Mrs. Budge."

⁓

She told him many of the pertinent details as they picked their way along the twisting path. Crossing her fingers, she related the bits she had been agonizing about since the day she wandered into the greenhouse.

"Wait just a minute." Jack stopped abruptly on the path. "Run that one by me again. You are telling me that Napoleon used Dimple and her greenhouse to grow marijuana?"

"Er, yes. That's what I'm telling you."

"How could she allow that in her own greenhouse?"

"He told her it was legal, for medicinal purposes only."

His eyebrows shot up. "And she believed that?"

"People ignore what they don't want to see, don't they? Oh, one other thing—there's a dog."

"A dog?"

The detective reached for his gun just as the huge creature came charging out of the greenhouse in front of Dimple.

"Hello, Detective Denny. This is Pepper. He's really a sweet dog; you don't need to shoot him. He keeps me company on my walks."

He looked unconvinced but holstered the weapon anyway. "Hello, Ms. Dent. I understand you are having some concerns about your greenhouse."

She shoved her hands into the pocket of her overalls. "Yes. You'll never believe it."

"I bet I won't," he muttered as he stepped past her

into the greenhouse. He surveyed the array of equipment and plants. The most mature plants were enormous now, towering over his head in spiky green confusion. It was as if they were in some gorgeous illicit tropical jungle, and Ruth wouldn't have been surprised if a parrot or spider monkey swooped down to scold them.

Slowly, he turned and stared at the two women standing behind him. He rubbed his hands over his stubbled chin and breathed deeply before he continued. "Ms. Dent, you had no idea that it was illegal to farm marijuana? Is that correct?"

She raised her chin. "Yes. I mean, no. Well, he told me it was legal to grow as long as it was sold to sick people. He said they were researching ways to make it into a medicine for asthma. That sounded very helpful. My cousin Alice has asthma, and she never could make it through a full season of lacrosse. She was an excellent player, too."

Jack's eyes widened as he tried to follow the conversational segue.

"Uh, Dimple," Ruth interjected, "why did you keep it a secret?"

She bowed her head sadly, the fringe of hair covering her face, her baggy denim stretched over the tiny bulb of a tummy. A tear trickled down her face and plopped onto one of her high-top sneakers. "He told me to keep it quiet to discourage the curious, and I did. He left the cultivation entirely to me."

Jack cleared his throat and continued in a gentler tone. "And you weren't the least bit suspicious that it wasn't being used the way he told you?"

"No," she said, raising her chin. "I'm very good at following directions, not so good at asking questions."

"And when we sweep this place for prints, yours will be all over these flats, but not his, I take it?"

Dimple nodded silently.

His gaze swept over the greenery one last time. "Orthodontists never run into this stuff."

"What?" Ruth and Dimple asked at once.

"Nothing. I'm going to need to talk to you some more about this, ladies. For the time being, let's just step outside and close the door."

They walked into the cool outside air.

"So," he said incredulously, "there's a nice marijuana plantation right up Finny's Nose. The plants are pretty lush. Must be the climate," he mused.

"No, it all depends on the nutrient additives," Dimple corrected soberly.

The detective sighed again, and Ruth patted him on the shoulder.

32

*W*hen he arrived, she was applying paint in short, angry strokes to the naked canvas. Her smock was covered with speckles of every color, and her cheek was smudged with orange.

"Hello, Meena." He had shortened her name because Benjamina was too many syllables, and he just couldn't call a woman whom he had kissed Ben.

"Hi."

"You're angry about something."

"Why would you say something like that?" she snapped.

"Because you're painting the entire thing in red."

"I am not. For your information, Officer, this is vermilion, dusty carmine, and glossy ocher. Not a single red."

"A red by any other name." He wedged himself in a student desk and stuck his legs out in front of him, one scuffed boot crossed over the other. "Since you're not mad, I guess these roses on the floor must have been dropped by accident."

"I guess so."

He was slouching casually, trying desperately to see the print on the white card sticking out of the crumpled blossoms.

She whirled around to face him, paintbrush pointing from her hand like a dagger. "If I was mad, I would be mad at me. Do you know why?"

He was pretty sure this was a rhetorical question, so he decided not to hazard an answer.

"Because I am a strong woman. I should be able to

take care of myself, shouldn't I? If someone is harassing me, I can take care of it without the help of a brawny man."

"Is someone harassing you?" He spoke very calmly.

"No. I said if someone did. And anyway, what would you do if someone was?"

"I'd take care of it for you."

"Exactly. That's exactly what I'm talking about. Do you see? I can take care of myself."

He paused for a moment before answering. "I don't understand your viewpoint, but I can empathize with your feelings of frustration."

She narrowed her eyes. "You went to one of those sensitivity training things for work, didn't you?"

"Is this when I am supposed to send an 'I' message or mirror your feelings? I always get that mixed up."

She collapsed into a chair and banged her head on the top of the desk.

"So," he resumed, "is someone harassing you?"

"What would you do about it? Never mind, I know. You'd punch his lights out, right?"

"Of course not. I'm a cop," he said, rubbing his chin, smiling. "You never go for the face; it leaves too many bruises."

She stared at him, openmouthed. Then she got up, took off her smock, and grabbed a shoulder bag from her desk drawer.

"Where are you going?

"To find some chocolate."

"Mind if I go along?"

"Only if you don't give me any more idiotic 'I' messages."

"I understand your feelings completely," he said, ducking

the flying shoulder bag.

Ruth was fairly sure she was going to be incarcerated momentarily. She couldn't think of any other reason Jack would summon her to the police station on this Wednesday, the day after their field trip to Dimple's greenhouse. She felt so tired, so very tired, as she shifted uneasily on the waiting room bench. It was ironic that a person who never even got a speeding ticket was going to jail for befriending a strange woman who concealed drug cultivation from the police.

Dejectedly she shoved her hands into her pockets. Her fingers closed around a paper. The baby picture. She slipped it from the envelope and squinted at it.

"Who is that? She's cute."

Her head jerked up so quickly her neck cracked. "Oh, hello, Red. Actually, it's a he. I'm not positive, but I think it's Napoleon Prinn's son."

Red looked at the photo, her face a picture of surprise. "Wow. A son. I didn't know he had one. How did you find it?"

"It belonged to the baby's mother. She's in a mental hospital in Miramar." She returned the photo to her pocket. "What are you doing here?"

Red hiked up the legs of her overalls and plopped onto the bench next to Ruth. "Oh, I just wanted to ask the coppers if I can get out of this town. I'm tired of fog and gravel. I want to go home."

"What did he say?"

"He asked me to stay until the end of the week." She yawned widely enough for Ruth to see her tonsils. "I guess I'm stuck here for two more days."

"What is going to happen to the statue? Of Broken Bird."

"It's going to stay right here in the heart of Finny until all this investigation stuff is over. Then, who knows? Maybe it will go back to the Shaum. I'm not really sure." Her tone was bitter. "I just want to go home, at this point, and put Finny and Napoleon far behind me."

"You must miss New York, being cooped up in this small town for so long."

"The town's okay. It's the people; they all know everything about everything. There is no privacy here. And the fog is so depressing."

The door to Jack's office opened and the detective came out.

"Hi, Mrs. Budge. I've been waiting for you." She couldn't read his face. "Thanks for coming by, Ms. Finchley."

Walking into his cluttered office, Ruth extended her hands and closed her eyes as she plopped into a chair. "I'm turning myself in," she said. After a few seconds of no wrist shackling, she opened an eye. "Aren't you going to arrest me? Isn't that why you hauled me in?"

He was grinning widely, shaking his head from side to side. "You watch way too much television." He laughed aloud. "I just need you to sign your statement about finding the body in the fountain. But now that I'm thinking of it, I'm going to pay a visit to K and K Nursery in Half Moon Bay. We think that's where the fuchsias were purchased. Maybe you could come along, since you know more about these plant suckers than I do."

"Oh. Well. Sure. Okay. Sure. When did you want to go?" Relief flooded through her, restoring oxygen flow to the deprived muscles.

"Are you free tomorrow?" He leaned forward, scowling ferociously. "I think you'd better say yes, or I'll have to bust you for interfering with a murder investigation."

"Well, when you put it that way. . ."

33

*R*oper Mackey was four yards away from Benjamina's office door when he stopped. It was hard not to eavesdrop on the shouting.

"It's not arrogance, Benjamina. I can tell when a woman is interested. I can tell when a woman is enjoying a kiss," Toulouse said.

"Enjoying? I could press assault charges for your behavior the night of the ball."

"No one would believe you."

There was incredulous silence for a moment.

The man continued, "You are a beautiful, cultured woman. You need a man with education and ambition. Someone who is going places, not some redneck cop who can open a beer bottle with his teeth."

Roper grimaced, leaning one shoulder against the wall.

"What I need and who I see is none of your business. The only thing you need to know is, I do not want to see you, talk to you, smell you, or otherwise share the same air you breathe in this lifetime!" She was practically shrieking by now.

Roper ducked back into a corner as he heard footsteps.

"You'll change your mind, Ms. Pena. I'll be waiting."

Roper watched the man's navy blue back with disgust.

Benjamina's voice reverberated in the close hallway. "And for your information, I've gotten better kisses from my springer spaniel!" A coffee cup crashed into bits against the office door, sending rivulets of brown liquid dribbling to the floor.

Roper waited a few moments until he was sure there

were no other porcelain projectiles coming before approaching Benjamina's office.

"I didn't know you had a springer spaniel," he said.

She sat rigidly upright at the desk, hands clenched into fists, cheeks pink with rage, lips parted. "I always wanted one."

He nodded, walking behind the desk to take her in his arms.

34

The drive to Half Moon Bay would have been breathtaking if she had remembered her Dramamine. As it was, the route along Highway 1 was just winding enough to tint the cliff sides and thundering surf a faint shade of vomit green. Philip had always tried to plan vacations on very straight roads to very flat places with frequent stops for saltines and tepid water.

Jack glanced over occasionally on the straighter patches of road. "Are you okay? You look green around the gills."

She nodded. "Fine. I forgot to tell you I get seasick, airsick, carsick, and elevator sick. I don't travel well. But I never leave home without a plastic bag, so you don't need to worry about the upholstery."

He laughed. "I wasn't worried. You just let me know if I need to stop."

"Okay."

They traveled in relative silence until they began a gradual decent into the fertile valley colored with acres of young Christmas trees and rusty-hued mums. Jack drummed his thumbs on the steering wheel and shifted in his seat.

"There's something I've been meaning to talk to you about." He noted her uneasy glance. "Not related to manufacturing of an illegal substance. A personal thing."

She relaxed. "Fire away."

"Well, you remember the night I barged in on you to talk about the Heston Blue thing?" He waited for her nod. "After Ulysses and I finished our knock-down-drag-out on the hood of my car, you remember what happened? With Paul?"

"Of course I do. I'll never forget that giggle. Has he begun to talk at all?"

"No," he said, slowing for a sharp bend in the road, "that was it, just the giggle. Anyway, I was thinking that somehow he seems to connect with your birds. At least, he did then."

He turned to look at her, his eyes crinkled in frustration and despair. "I have to reach him, Ruth. I have to find the happy boy I had before Lacey died. I know he's in there somewhere. I'm not much good at this daddy thing, but I'm the best he's got."

She nodded gently. "You bring him over anytime, as much as you want. They aren't the most loving of companions, but if we fill Paul's pockets with onion rings, they'll follow him to the ends of the earth."

He laughed heartily and thanked her.

In spite of her uncooperative stomach, she enjoyed the conversation and the lush view as they headed away from the coastline. The valley was green and peppered with purple and yellow wildflowers. Ranch land suddenly shifted to a packed gravel path, which led the way to a split-rail fence that separated the nursery from the surrounding pasture. She opened the window to breathe in the scent of damp soil.

They pulled into the gravel lot of K and K Nursery. The building that greeted them was wooden and leaned somewhat starboard, with long, low windows and a peeling door trying desperately to part ways with its hinges. This was the office building. The entire property sprawled over twenty loamy acres and housed the most advanced greenhouses money could buy.

"The K and K stands for Kermit and Kermit. They are known for growing rare and exotic types of flowering plants. Four fuchsias matching the types delivered to Prinn the week before his murder were sold from this nursery to an out-of-towner."

"How did you find that out?"

"Exceptional police work."

She raised a newly sprouted eyebrow.

"Blind, stupid luck didn't hurt, either. Nate found a piece of the fancy foil stuff they use to dress up the plastic pots stuck inside Dimple's Mary Jane fuchsia. It was just a scrap, but he remembered seeing something like it, so he took it home to his wife. She used to work for a nursery wholesale supplier when she was in college. She recognized the swirly designs on the foil. It's a type used by only a few nurseries because it's apparently expensive and comes on big rolls that you cut yourself. Most places buy the cheaper stuff that's precut. Then it was just a matter of making some phone calls."

The interior of the shop was dark and cool. Kermit was not at all what Ruth had expected. Mentally slapping herself, she realized she had been expecting green flippers and ping-pong-ball eyes. Actually, the old man's eyes did look a little ping-pongish as he scrutinized them from behind lenses rivaling the Hubble telescope's.

His skin was as leathery. The hair standing straight out from the top of his head looked like new straw, and his eyes were a startling Play-Doh blue. He looked at them over the top of his glasses.

"You must be the cop. And—?" He pointed a crusty finger at Ruth.

"Yes, Detective Denny, and this is Ruth Budge. You are Mr. Narvik, Senior?"

"Uh-huh. You wanted to know about some fuchsias."

"Yes." Jack consulted his notebook. "Common names Heston Blue, Mary Jane, and Payoff."

"Mmmm. Some fella called in the orders. Saturday was the first two."

"The first two? They weren't ordered at the same time?"

"No. Fella ordered the Heston Blues. Said he couldn't pick it up until late 'cause he was coming in from out of town. Dropped his payment in the mail slot, and we left 'em on the porch for him after closing time."

"That was a week ago Saturday?"

"Yes, Saturday the eighth."

That must have been the plant she saw Donnelly taking to the trash heap, Ruth thought. The other came sailing out of the greenhouse door.

"How did he pay for it?"

"Cash. It wasn't cheap, either. We charge extra for special orders. It isn't easy to come by some of these fuchsias. I had to call around for Payoff. Not many people ask for that one."

Jack was scribbling furiously. "What about the other two orders?"

"Two days after he picked up the first batch—that'd be Tuesday the eleventh, I guess—he called again, asking for Mary Jane and Payoff. I told him I couldn't have Payoff until Friday but he could pick up the Mary Jane the next day. He dropped the cash in the slot Wednesday evening, sometime after seven o'clock. That's closing time. We did the same thing with the last plant on Thursday night. Put it out on the porch after quitting time."

Ruth did some quick mental math. Last Friday was the fourteenth, the day Prinn was killed.

"Did this person contact you again after he picked up the plant Thursday night?"

"No. Only saw him the once."

Ruth looked at Jack, whose lips had parted in astonishment. "You saw him?" she said.

Kermit was enjoying the drama he had created. He rubbed his nose thoughtfully and stretched his shoulders before answering. "Sure. I stuck around late one night, doing some book work, and I heard him on the porch. I poked my head out to be neighborly."

They both stared at him, and she thought surely her own eyes must be the size of ping pong balls. "Did you folks want some coffee or something?"

"No. What did he look like?"

Ruth could feel Jack's agitation increasing.

"Hard to say. It was almost dark and real foggy."

Kermit's comments were interrupted by the phone on his desk. He picked up the ancient receiver. "Yeah? Oh man, I already told you. Uh-huh, well, I guess I could. Got a pencil?" He covered the mouthpiece and gestured for them to sit in the Naugahyde chairs.

Ruth sat; Jack didn't move.

Though she could only see the detective's back, she noticed a distinct flush creeping up his neck from under the collar.

"Well, that's because you are an idiot." Kermit covered the mouthpiece again. "My brother can't keep a recipe straight to save his soul."

By the time he hung up, Jack looked as if he were going to explode into millions of frustrated bits. "You said you saw him." His words were clipped and low. "What did he look like, Mr. Narvik?"

"Who?"

"The man who picked up the plants!"

"Oh, him. Well, it's hard to say. He was all muffled up, long coat, knit cap. Strong guy, though, hauled those plants up in no time, and they ain't feathers, either, when they just been watered."

"Did you talk to him?"

"Not much. I asked him what he wanted the plants for. He said it was for a collector friend. Said he was just visiting the coast, never been here before. I asked him what he thought about our coastal fog. He said he was getting accustomed to the dark. He was taller than me by a head. I think that was about it."

"Was there anything unusual about his voice?"

"No. Kinda gravelly, I guess. Like he had a cold. Spoke real quiet."

"Did you notice anything else? Eye color? Hair color? Age? Any distinguishing marks?"

"Mmmm. No. As I said, it was dark. He was all covered up. That's all I noticed."

Jack pocketed his notebook. "Thank you, Mr. Narvik. Here's my card. Please call me if you think of anything else."

"You're welcome. Come again."

Back in the car, Ruth and Jack were quiet for a while. Finally, Jack cleared his throat and twisted the key in the ignition.

"Well, Ruth? Do you have any thoughts worth sharing?"

She hesitated for a fraction of a second. "No. I don't think so."

He eyed her sharply. "There's something. What is it?"

"Oh, it's nothing. Just something about the conversation struck a familiar chord with me, but I can't think what it is. Maybe if I just stew on it for a while, something will come to me."

As the miles wound by, nothing came but queasiness.

35

It wasn't the crash of Alva's newspaper that woke her up Friday morning but rather the tense murmuring voices wafting up from her front porch to her open bedroom window. Wrapping a nubby purple robe around her, she padded down the stairs and peered through the peephole, directly at a very large person's chin. It was attached to the grave-looking face of Monk. Standing next to him nervously zipping and unzipping his jacket was Alva.

"It's a terrible thing, Ruth. Terrible." Alva's eyes began to tear up, and his lips trembled. "I can't feature who coulda done it."

Monk patted him gently on the shoulder. "It's okay, Alva. You did the right thing coming to get me. I can take it from here. Why don't you go along now?" He spoke gently, as if talking to a confused child.

Alva wiped a sleeve under his bulbous nose. "Okay. I just can't feature it." He shuffled off down the driveway, muttering to himself.

She was beginning to feel a rising tide of panic. "Monk. What is going on? What has happened?"

Monk shifted his weight uneasily from one huge foot to the other. He was wearing an apron stained with brown streaks and smelling of bouillabaisse, and a slotted spoon was shoved in the back pocket of his jeans. "Something bad has happened. I have to believe it was some crackpot, probably last night I think, or it could have been early this morning. . ."

"What?" she practically shrieked. "Just tell me already.

I'm going to jump out of my skin."

"You'd better come with me."

He led her to the side of the house. It took her a few minutes to spot anything unusual. She saw something white lying at the bottom of the gate. At first she thought it looked like a bundle of laundry or maybe a pillowcase. As she got closer she stopped dead in her tracks, and her hands flew to her mouth.

"Oh no," she whispered, her stomach convulsing.

"He's not dead, just hurt. Alva saw him on his route. He didn't know what to do, so he came to get me."

Ulysses was sprawled on the ground, feathers draped in disarray like a white handkerchief flung on the ground. His eyes were open, little feet sticking up in the air. The muscles around his throat thrummed weakly.

She knelt down beside him, stroking his wing feathers gently. "It's okay, my friend. You're going to be okay." She noticed the piece of cardboard sticking out from under his body. Sliding it out, she read the one-word scrawl.

STOP.

"Stop? Stop what? Who could have done this?" She felt like crying, but no tears would come: Her eyes burned instead.

Monk looked at her helplessly. "I don't know. Do you suppose it has something to do with all the strangeness around here lately?"

The world was spinning, drowning her again and again.

She looked up abruptly, gazing at him without seeing. "I think someone wants me to stop looking for him. And I know who that someone is."

"I'll help you. Whatever you need. Let me help you, please." He opened his arms to fold her inside. This time, she did not push him away.

———

It was nearly two hours before she returned to her kitchen, still wearing the fuzzy purple robe. Nathan Katz had arrived to take her statement, followed a few minutes later by Jack. Ulysses had been delivered to the vet, who promised to do what she could for him. Monk said he would stay for a while at the vet's office.

Jack told her they would find the person who did it but didn't think that bird assault was probably very high on the Finny Police Department priority list. Unless, of course, the attacker of birds and gallery owners was one and the same. The police would be doing a drive-by check of her house every hour or two until they knew for sure.

The rest of the day passed in a blur of confusion. She did her chores robotically, feeding, cleaning, and trying to comfort herself and the birds. Afternoon morphed into evening, and still she could not shake her state of shock.

She could picture in her mind's eye how it was done. The perpetrator had gone to the gate, probably with some food treat, and the birds had come running. Ulysses was the most aggressive, and he had, no doubt, pushed his way to the front. It would have been an easy thing then to open the gate a crack and grab the bird as he edged through. She wondered if he had been surprised when the hands began hurting him. Quickly she shook her head to dislodge the disturbing mental picture.

She knew in her heart that it was Heston Blue. She could feel the anger and fear in that one simple word. *Stop.* He knew she had been to see Bun, maybe even knew she found out his secrets from the library book. What else did he know? He was close, watching. Maybe even right now.

Shivering, she checked the locks for the fourth time, then went upstairs to bed. Monk called again to check on her. The vet was hopeful about Ulysses' recovery, he reported. She thanked him and told him she was fine. As much as she didn't want to admit it, she looked forward to his frequent phone calls.

She lay down on the bed and folded her hands. Lately her prayers had begun to sound different. Maybe it was just a deeper level of desperation. Or maybe it was the fact that she had been drawn inextricably into the lives of the people around her for a brief moment. She wanted to feel again. Something, anything. Even the current turmoil was better than the awful numbness.

"Lord, I am not sure You're listening. I'm not sure of anything anymore. But I am going to ask You one more time. Help me, Lord. Help me crawl out of this dark hole. Help me turn my face to the light and feel Your loving embrace again. I am so tired, Lord. I am so tired of this life. Please show me a better one."

Pulling the covers over her head, she cried bitterly until she drifted off to sleep.

In her dreams she was running, chased by a dark figure in a trench coat with a bird in each pocket. Just as he reached her, grabbing at her hair, she awoke, dripping with sweat and breathing raggedly. It took a split second for her to remember. Even squeezing her eyes shut did not erase the picture of her maimed bird.

Ruth hauled herself out of bed and waited until the hammering in her chest subsided. Her glance wandered over the familiar items on her dresser. The fat bristled hairbrush, a beautiful bottle of eau de something that she never used, and the photo Jack had given her of Heston Blue.

The baby gazed out at her from the gray background, eyes wide and round. She fished around in her top drawer and found a magnifying glass. Squinting, she examined the figure closely. The dotted pajamas hugged the baby's plump arms, flexed with the effort of holding his body up. How did such a tiny thing become a cold-blooded killer? She looked more closely.

Her breath froze in her lungs as she peered through the lens.

The tiny dots weren't dots. They were hearts. Hearts, with a tiny flower inside each one.

Hearts? On a baby boy?

She stood there with the magnifying glass gripped tightly between her fingers. It seemed as if she were at the top of a high cliff, looking down. The thought of looking over the edge terrified her.

She thought of Benjamina; the strong, beautiful woman who was not afraid of challenges, of life. Ruth was not strong, not beautiful, not accomplished, but she felt something new welling up inside her; a feeling of strength that started at her cold bare feet and grew as it rose until she felt as though it would explode out of her. She was not strong, not beautiful, but maybe she could be that other woman, make her real for one moment in time. Maybe God would give her a chance.

She put the magnifying glass down very carefully.

Tomorrow morning she would finish her conversation with Bun Zimmerman.

36

By the time she reached the Zimmerman cottage, it was almost eight o'clock, and the morning chill froze her to the bone. Her knock sounded loud, echoing down the quiet street.

It was completely silent, so she banged again. Finally, she heard soft scuffling noises of someone heaving herself up to the peephole.

The door opened a crack and Wanda peeked out. "Ruth?" She opened the door wider, hand on her hip, flipping her ponytail in irritation. "What are you doing whacking on my door?"

"I need to see your mother."

She heard the sound of Bun's wheelchair bumping up to the front door.

"What is it, Ruth? I thought we were finished."

"I want to know about Heston Blue. The truth this time. I'm not leaving until you tell me."

Bun's eyes widened for a split second before she said, "I see. Come inside, then."

Wanda, in a state of bewilderment, opened the door and led her into a stale-smelling front room. The walls were marred with wheelchair scuffs; a candy dish on the table was filled with stony-looking pretzels. It had the musty smell of an attic or trunk that has finally been opened after years of neglect.

"You need to go, Wanda. This is a private matter," Bun said quietly to her daughter.

"What do you mean, a private matter? This is my

house, too. I have a right to know what goes on under my own roof."

"Who pays the mortgage? Do you want to talk about that right now? Right here?"

Wanda ground her teeth and grunted angrily before she turned on her heel and stalked out.

"Now. What do you want to know?"

"I want to know the truth. It's incredibly important."

"I don't see why it matters now."

"It matters. You've got to tell me." Ruth realized her voice was getting louder.

The old woman took a deep breath and sat ramrod straight in her wheelchair. "All right, then. What do you want to know?"

"Heston Blue is a girl, isn't she?"

Bun exhaled dejectedly. "Yes."

"You helped deliver the baby. You were there. Why the lies? To me, and on the birth certificate?"

"I didn't think it could hurt anyone. Jenny was so desperate to keep Napoleon. She thought he would stay if she had his son. When the baby was born, she was heartbroken; she thought sure it was a boy." Bun plucked absently at a hair protruding from under her chin. "She figured if he would just come back, meet the baby, he would decide to stay and be a father for her. Poor, stupid girl."

"So you falsified the birth certificate, didn't you?"

"She wanted to send him a copy of the birth certificate. To prove she'd had a baby, a son. I figured that once her harebrained scheme failed, I could slip into the records office and change the document. Or maybe at the baby's first checkup the doctor would notice and think it was a mistake. A typo. She was just so desperate."

Bun gazed out the window. "I wanted to help her somehow. She had a really terrible life, always got the short end of the stick. Anyway, the whole mess didn't accomplish a thing because he never came back. When I went back to do the three-week checkup, they were gone. Jenny, Heston, and all their worldly belongings. I never heard from them again. I figured it was best to leave well enough alone."

Bun sat still, looking at the floor. Then, "Do you know where Jenny is? Is she still alive?"

"Yes. She's alive, living in a mental hospital not far from here." She tried to be gentle. "She's pretty confused. The doctors say she's happy, but not aware of the real world."

Tears gathered in the old woman's eyes, and she looked down into her lap. She wiped a sleeve across her lips. "Do you think Heston killed her father?"

"All I know is someone with a connection to Heston Blue is involved in two murders." She thought for a split second about Ulysses and shuddered, hoping she was not destined to be the third. "I've got to go." She reached out to grasp the woman's hand. "You did the right thing."

She glanced back and saw Bun watching her run down the street, into the gathering fog.

Ruth paced up and down her hallway and in and out of her kitchen, trying to unmuddle the muddle in her head. Her lunch lay untouched on the table. It was a case of way too much information for some compromised neuropathways, she thought. Heston Blue was not a man. Then who picked up the fuchsias from Kermit Narvik at his nursery? Something about the nursery owner's conversation was jiggling at the corner of her mind. Something familiar.

After a quarter mile more of hallway pacing, she gave up, placing one phone call before she went outside to gather her flock. They were nervous, vibrating with anxiety. As she let them out the gate and onto the sidewalk, they darted forward and then fell back in a confused acrobatic frenzy. They all needed a good walk to clear their bird brains, hers included.

She waved a hello to Alva as he pedaled a dilapidated purple bicycle complete with a wicker basket attached to the handlebars.

"Takin' a walk, sweet cheeks?" he croaked.

"Just trying to clear my mind. I think I'll head up to the gallery."

"Okey dokey," he called, wobbling away down the slope.

The air was cool, on the way to cold, heavy with moisture from the increasing fog as the day wound its way to a close. Her steps took her up the gentle slope out of town.

The gallery was quiet and very closed looking, but the front doors were unlocked. She walked into the front foyer and listened: no sounds of human habitation, so she wandered down the hallway toward the west wing and slowly pulled open the double doors and entered the showroom. It took a few seconds of blinking to accustom her eyes to the dimly lit space.

It hit her like a backhanded slap.

Snatches of a conversation in her own living room came back to her from the far reaches of her memory.

"How does that poem go? The one about the neighbor holding the lamp until her friend's eyes adjust to the dark?"

She had been unable to recall the exact lines of Dickinson's poem before, but now they echoed in her head.

"We grow accustomed to the Dark, when Light is put away. . ."

Kermit said that the person who picked up the plants that night was strong, rough voiced.

"I asked him what he thought about our coastal fog. He said he was getting accustomed to the dark."

The person who picked up the plants that night was Heston Blue all right, only Heston was a woman. A strong woman, with a gravelly voice, who knew Emily Dickinson poetry. The same woman who had sat in her house, reading Phillip's story.

Red Finchley.

Ruth was so completely stunned by her discovery that she did not hear the sound of the doors opening behind her.

"What are you doing here? I saw your birds outside when I was loading up some stuff."

"Oh, I—was—out for a walk." Her mind was racing.

" I wanted to see the piece again. *Broken Bird*." She walked quickly over to the statue, hoping her hammering heart wasn't visible on the skin side. There was an emergency exit door about five yards away.

Red followed along behind her. "What do you think of it?"

"I think it's just wonderful. Really. Wonderful."

Red looked at her closely, cocking her head slowly to one side. "You know, don't you?"

"Know what?" Ruth's mouth went dry.

Red lifted her chin, the kinks of red hair falling around her face like tangled snakes. "You know about me. I can see it in your face; you know it's mine."

Mine? She watched Red's face gazing in almost maternal admiration at the anguished figure of the young girl. Of course. She remembered a fictional scene between Benjamina and Roper.

"You're painting the entire thing in red.". . .

"For your information, Officer, this is vermilion, dusty carmine, and glossy ocher.". . .

"A red by any other name."

A red by any other name would be—a Carmine. Red was that Carmine.

"You're the sculptor?"

She folded her freckled arms. "That surprised you. So that isn't why you look so spooked." Her eyes bored into Ruth's face.

Ruth was suddenly aware of how strong Red looked.

"I see. You figured out the other little detail, too," Red said. "That I am really Heston Blue, Prinn's would-be son."

"I don't know what you are talking about. I'd better

go check on the birds."

Red/Heston took a step closer, her lips pressed into a thin line. "You know exactly what I'm talking about. You've been hustling all over this jerkwater town trying to find out about me, haven't you? You had to go digging around Bun Zimmerman. She told you, didn't she? Then I saw you with that photo, and I knew that you were getting close."

"Is that why you hurt my bird? You got scared?"

Red licked her lips uneasily. "I didn't want to hurt him, Ruth. I just wanted to send you a message. It got out of control when he started fighting me."

Ruth took a giant leap. "Is that what happened to Crew Donnelly? Did he find out about you, too?" She edged one step closer to the exit door.

"He was greedy. He saw me delivering a plant to darling Daddy's office and he wanted to know why. He said he would go right to Prinn if I didn't come clean, so I arranged to meet him in town at some ridiculously late hour.

"Do you know what he let slip? That Daddy was smuggling marijuana in the paintings. Can you believe that? The great art curator, a common smuggler. Donnelly figured that I was blackmailing Prinn for a share of the profits. I told him I didn't have a clue about any drugs. I was here on a personal matter. He didn't believe me because I wouldn't tell him who I was. He said he was going to go to Prinn anyway.

"Then he turned his back on me. I can't stand having someone turn their back on me."

Red shook her head slowly from side to side.

"I slammed him on the head with a chisel I had brought for protection. I didn't mean to kill him. At least I hadn't planned to. After I knocked him out, I just slid him into the fountain."

"You murdered him."

"Yeah." She looked surprised. "I guess I did."

"Why did you come to Finny, anyway? Why these mysterious plant deliveries?"

Red pushed a wad of hair away from her freckled cheek. Her eyelashes were so fair they seemed invisible. "I wanted to get back at him. To show him who I really was."

Her words were bitter. "He left before I was born. He never wanted anything to do with us. Even after my mother tried so hard to get him back, telling him I was a boy and all that. He turned his back on us and it drove my mother crazy." The last few words were almost unintelligible. "She doesn't even know who I am now."

"He came to New York. Is that when you saw him for the first time?" Ruth prodded, trying to keep the woman talking as she sidled another step toward the door.

"Yeah. I was floored. Mother told me about him before she completely lost it, so I sort of followed his career. Then one day, out of the blue, he walks into the Shaum. And what's more, my curator assigns me to give him the grand tour and help him select a piece.

"I couldn't get over it. My own father walks right into my life and doesn't have a clue who I am." She laughed harshly. "It was just so bizarre. That's when I got the idea. I was going to sell him my own work, then confront him at his gallery dedication and force him to admit that I am a pretty awesome sculptor for someone from such pitiful stock. My curator dedicated part of an exhibit to local talent, and my piece was already there, waiting. It was so easy to fabricate some press releases about the great Carmine to pique his interest. He was such a raging egomaniac, I just flattered him about his wonderful eye, and he bought everything I told him.

"It worked flawlessly until I got here. Then I had to go and get fancy." She snorted, rolling her eyes toward the ceiling. "I wanted to torture him. To send those plants to let him know his "son" was sniffing around. Just to see him squirm with guilt. It was stupid, I know."

She was lost in thought. "I was totally floored when Donnelly told me about the weed. I guess I was sort of disappointed in a way at first. I know that sounds weird. I always thought my father was scum, but I figured he really was a great curator, building his own gallery and everything. Then I find out he was padding his bottom line with drugs. I went ballistic. When I calmed down, I figured I would blackmail him into giving me a share in the gallery. I mean, what could he say? His own child an accomplished sculptor who just happens to know Daddy's little sideline?"

"So you ordered two more plants to scare him before you revealed yourself. Mary Jane and Payoff, wasn't it?"

"Yeah. Kind of clever, don't you think? I knew the plant nut would get the message." She paused. "I should have left town, but I had to finish my business with Daddy."

Ruth had only a few more steps to go to reach the door. She swallowed convulsively and continued. "What went wrong? Why did you kill him?"

There was silence for a moment. "I went to tell him. The night of the dedication." Her gaze became unfocused, her hands stroking the wooden rail. "I went to his office on some pretense of a last bit of paperwork. I had put the last fuchsia there earlier. He was so mad when he saw it, his face turned completely red." She giggled. "Anyway, I told him who I was. I told him that I was his daughter. I was the sculptor of his grand 'new addition.'

"Do you know what he did?"

Her eyes riveted on Ruth's, and the older woman could see years of pain and rejection there mingled with a profound rage.

"He laughed. He laughed so hard tears ran down his face. He said my pitiful attempts to get his attention had failed. He said he didn't care if I was his flesh and blood; he would never give me any part in his gallery."

Ruth was silent, imagining the awful scene. A grown woman trying to blackmail her father into acknowledging her existence.

"And things got out of hand again?"

"Yeah. I smashed the plant on that arrogant head. Then I left and ate crab bisque." She began a chuckling that gradually increased in strength and hysteria. "So I guess that means I've killed two people."

She stopped giggling and wiped her eyes. "And I guess that means I have to kill you, too. It's a funny thing about killing people. After you get over the novelty of it, it really isn't all that significant."

Ruth was no longer listening. Her body was taken over by a need that overcame her other five senses. She realized she desperately, unwaveringly, ferociously wanted to stay alive. Her body seemed suddenly bursting with all the feelings she had drowned out for the past two years.

In one brief moment of clarity, she knew that the life God had given her was precious, more than precious. She was more than a widow. More than a lonely person caring for homeless birds. She was loved and she mattered, with or without a husband. God had been there all along, even when she shut Him out. He gave her Jack, He gave her Monk, and she knew He would give her the strength to save herself.

Before Red finished with the last syllable, she flung herself at the panic bar on the door and made it outside. The girl pursued her in a flash.

Ruth was no match in strength or speed for the younger woman. Just before Red reached her, Ruth remembered the crumpled foil package in her pocket. Fingers scrabbling wildly, she tore open the bag of stale Fritos and hurled them into the air, shouting, "Treat!" with all the volume she could muster.

The birds reacted immediately, swarming around her, swallowing up the woman in their greedy haste.

Red tottered for a few seconds, yelping, before she fell over, grunting as she hit the ground. She scrambled to her feet again, but before she could resume her sprint, a voice halted her.

"Stop, Ms. Blue! Just stay right there, hands in front of you." Jack, gun drawn, stood between Ruth, the swarm of birds zinging crazily between the path, and the panting red-haired woman. Right behind him was a frantic Monk. Without taking his eyes off his quarry, Jack addressed a question over his shoulder to Ruth.

"Are you okay?"

Dragging herself upright, Ruth tried several times before the word "yes" actually came out.

"It's a good thing you called the station and told Nate that Heston and Red were one and the same." Jack circled around and cuffed Red's hands behind her back.

The look Red leveled at Ruth was filled with fury.

"How did you know to look for me here?" Ruth gasped, tearing her eyes away.

"A sweet old guy told me you were on your way to the gallery. Right before he asked me for candy," Jack said.

Monk enveloped her in a colossal hug. "Thank God." Tears shone in his eyes. "I could have lost you. Praise God, you're okay."

"Yes," she said, looking into his kind blue eyes. "Praise God."

The waves played a taunting game of tag with the birds, beckoning them with foamy fingers as the flock ran back and forth with undisguised zeal. Ruth watched without seeing them, her mind running amok through images of Red's anguish and her own mind-numbing fear the day before at the gallery.

Oddly, she could sympathize with the girl. Red had been dealt only rejection and pain in her life. She could relate to the feeling of betrayal. No, that was unfair to Phillip. It was not betrayal, not really. Just a shock, and maybe a way to know him again for a short while.

Her Sunday headache was gone by the time Monk picked her up for church that morning. It was his suggestion to spend some time at the beach later that day to "clear out her noggin." She watched him chasing after an errant bird. He looked up from his pursuit and waved at her. Praise God for this second chance at life. And perhaps a special man to live it with.

"I just can't imagine what this world is coming to," Ellen exclaimed, stalking up with her boxer at her side. The dog edged menacingly toward the birds until he got a good look at six pairs of hostile yellow eyes glaring at him. He wisely backed away, cowering behind her legs.

"It certainly is a tragedy."

"Here I am, trying to be friendly, giving that terrible woman a visitor's library card. What does it get me? Do you know that little felon checked out three items before she got busted? Goodness knows where they are now.

We'll probably never see them again. That's a crime, I'll have you know. And she owes two dollars and sixty-five cents in fines."

Ellen marched off down the beach, mumbling to herself, leaving Ruth shaking her head and chuckling in disbelief. As she wiped her eyes, a blur of running feet sent her birds scattering in every direction.

Jack caught Paul up in his arms. "I thought you might be here."

"Hi, Jack. Hello, Paul." The boy buried his head in his father's jacket.

"Are you doing okay?" he asked.

"I think so. I was just sitting here thinking about Red. You know, I really don't think she meant it personally, trying to murder me, I mean."

"That's a healthy way to look at it, I guess. I'm just glad you are here to talk about it."

She smiled. "Me, too." She looked at the tiny boy in Jack's arms.

Paul began to squirm and contort himself until his father plopped him onto the sand. He ran directly for the gaggle.

Jack yelled over the crashing waves, "Don't chase the birds, buddy. You'll scare them."

Paul had already soaked his sweatpants up to the knees and grimed one elbow when he fell in the soggy sand. He turned to look at his father. Ruth gasped. His cheeks were flushed and eyes dancing as he flapped his own arms in wild delight.

Tears glistened in Jack's eyes.

Gently she squeezed his shoulder. "Let them play," she said.

He was rolling code three seconds after the call came in to dispatch. A woman, being assaulted by three males, begging for help before the call was cut off.

Why hadn't he been more conscious of the danger? He'd been so focused on Toulouse that he hadn't anticipated that the thugs who laid him out that day with the bat might come back for Benjamina.

His tires squealed in her driveway, and he pounded up to the front door, his partner Greeney right behind him.

They were just in time to see a man vaulting out the open kitchen window. Greeney took off through the window, and Roper went room by room.

He found her in the guest room. She was lying facedown on the floor in a puddle of blood—her long black hair fanned out around her head and shoulders.

He knelt down.

"It's me, Meena. Roper. Can you hear me, baby?" His fingers were clammy and trembling as he pushed her hair aside and felt for a pulse. "Please let her be alive."

That was it. Ruth had searched every nook and cranny, checked every file on his computer. Nothing. Not a single sentence more. She pulled off the sweater she had not bothered to remove after the beach outing.

She felt an unreasonable anger rising in her chest, and this time she didn't try to stop it. How could he leave her with this unfinished story? This unfinished life? She would never know how it was supposed to end.

Red's words came back to her. *"Why don't you finish it?"*

Why?

Because it wasn't her dream.

Because she hadn't even known it was his.

The loose threads would torment her forever.

Unless.

She sat motionless for a very long time.

As if watching another person, she saw herself reach out and turn on the computer. It glowed a comforting blue, cursor blinking blandly.

How would it end? Would the woman bleed to death on the guest room floor?

Why not? Why not?

People died. Husbands, fathers, lovers. They left suddenly, with no tender good-byes or finishing of dreams. They left behind little children and empty houses. Quiet empty houses for quiet empty people.

The cursor blinked insistently. Why shouldn't Benjamina die and leave him alone?

Ruth thought for a long minute, weighting the scales with sorrow and sweetness. She was filled with a long-forgotten peace, and she knew how blessed she was to be there to make the decision.

She began to type.

He stilled every nerve, every breath, feeling for a pulse. Nothing. He moved fingers slippery with blood ever so slightly. There it was, a ragged, unsteady fluttering, like the beating of tiny wings.

Dimple sat on the rugged boulder alongside the path, studying her toes in the late Sunday sun. She looked almost childlike, except for the swelling around her middle. The noisy squabble was almost upon her before she looked up.

"Hello, Ruth," she said over the cacophony.

Reading lips more than hearing the words, Ruth replied, "Hi. How are you?"

She considered this as the feathery flood swept past her on the way to the pond. "I am well. I wanted to ask you something. I knew you would be walking the birds today here, so I've been waiting for you."

That surprised her.

"I need to go to the hospital for a check of the baby. The doctor is going to take a picture of it. I forget what he said it was called."

"A sonogram, I think."

"Yes, that's it. A sonogram. Don't you think that's amazing? A picture, a portrait, inside. The doctor says you can even see a tiny heart beating."

"That is amazing. A miracle, in fact." Ruth looked sadly at the woman. Amazing—a child within a child. All the same, perhaps it was better to be the product of a mind untouched by cynicism and doubt. But not untouched by grief, she thought, remembering Dimple's wail when Napoleon's body was discovered.

"The doctor said to bring a friend to the appointment and later to go to the classes with me, the birthing classes. Will you?"

"Me?" She was flabbergasted. "But surely you have other friends, other people who. . .your father, maybe?"

"My father says he is not my father anymore. I think that means I must be an orphan with living parents. Can you be that? An orphan with living parents?"

She stared at her, thinking of another young woman

whose parents had left her orphaned, too.

"I am alone, Ruth."

She looked at the little round face, capped with curls. It was ridiculous to consider. The woman was a stranger. There was no way she could do what Dimple asked.

A soft whisper of warmth spread inside her. The words of Dickinson's poem came to her again.

"*We grow accustomed to the Dark—when Light is put away—As when the Neighbor holds the Lamp to witness her Good-bye.*"

She thought about the wild set of circumstances that had brought her to this place, this moment. She thought about Dimple's baby. About Red. About Philip. About Monk. About the precious love that never left her.

Either the darkness alters—or something in the sight adjusts itself to Midnight—and Life steps almost straight.

After a long while, she said quietly, "We will go together, Dimple."

With a deep sigh, Dimple stood and straightened her trailing skirt. "Tomorrow, then. We will go tomorrow."

Ruth watched her drift away, the late afternoon sun catching the colors on her dress.

"Yes," she murmured, "tomorrow."

Turning her face toward the sun, she gathered her flock and started on the path for home.

Dana Mentink resides in sunny California where the climate is mild and the cheese is divine. She enjoys performing in mystery dinner theater and devouring books from her favorite authors. In between juggling an elementary teaching career, two beautiful girls, one husband, and a dog with social anxiety troubles, Dana enjoys writing mysteries and inspirational fiction.

You may correspond with this author by writing:
Dana Metink
Author Relations
PO Box 721
Uhrichsville, OH 44683

A Letter to Our Readers

Dear Reader:
In order to help us satisfy your quest for more great mystery stories, we would appreciate it if you would take a few minutes to respond to the following questions. We welcome your comments and read each form and letter we receive. When completed, please return to:

Fiction Editor
Heartsong Presents—MYSTERIES!
PO Box 721
Uhrichsville, Ohio 44683

Did you enjoy reading *Trouble Up Finny's Nose* by Dana Mentink?

Very much! I would like to see more books like this! The one thing I particularly enjoyed about this story was:

_____

_____

_____

Moderately. I would have enjoyed it more if:

_____

_____

_____

Are you a member of the HP—MYSTERIES! Book Club?
Yes   No

If no, where did you purchase this book?

_____

Please rate the following elements using a scale of 1 (poor) to 10 (superior):

___ Main character/sleuth   ___ Romance elements

___ Inspirational theme   ___ Secondary characters

___ Setting   ___ Mystery plot

How would you rate the cover design on a scale of 1 (poor) to 5 (superior)? _____

What themes/settings would you like to see in future **Heartsong Presents—MYSTERIES!** selections? _____

_____

_____

_____

Please check your age range:
- ○ Under 18   ○ 18–24
- ○ 25–34   ○ 35–45
- ○ 46–55   ○ Over 55

Name: _____

Occupation: _____

Address: _____

E-mail address: _____

┌─Heartsong Presents—MYSTERIES!─┐

Any 8 Titles
for $32!
A 20%
Savings!

Great Mysteries
at a Great Price!
Purchase Any Title for
Only $4.97 Each!

HEARTSONG PRESENTS—MYSTERIES TITLES AVAILABLE NOW:

__HPM1 *Death on a Deadline*, C. Lynxwiler
__HPM2 *Murder in the Milk Case*, C. Speare
__HPM3 *The Dead of Winter*, N. Mehl
__HPM4 *Everybody Loved Roger Harden*, C. Murphey
__HPM5 *Recipe for Murder*, L. Harris
__HPM6 *The Mysterious Incidents at Lone Rock*, R. K. Pillai
__HPM7 *Trouble Up Finny's Nose*, D. Mentink
__HPM8 *Homicide at Blue Heron Lake*, S. P. Davis & M. Davis

Heartsong Presents—MYSTERIES provide romance and faith
interwoven among the pages of these fun whodunits. Written by the
talented and brightest authors in this genre, such as Christine Lynxwiler,
Cecil Murphey, Nancy Mehl, Dana Mentink, Candice Speare, and
many others, these cozy tales are sure to challenge your mind, warm your
heart, touch your spirit—and put your sleuthing skills to the test.

Not all titles may be available at time of order.
If outside the U.S. please call
740-922-7280 for shipping charges.

SEND TO: **Heartsong Presents—Mysteries** Readers' Service
P.O. Box 721, Uhrichsville, Ohio 44683

Please send me the items checked above. I am enclosing $_____
(please add $3.00 to cover postage per order. OH add 7% tax. WA
add 8.5%). Send check or money order—no cash or C.O.D.s, please.
To place a credit card order, call 1-740-922-7280.

NAME _____

ADDRESS _____

CITY/STATE _____ ZIP_____

HEARTSONG
PRESENTS
MYSTERIES

Think you can outwit clever sleuths or unravel twisted plots?
If so, it's time to match your mystery-solving skills
against the lovable sleuths of
Heartsong Presents—MYSTERIES!

You know the feeling—you're so engrossed in a book that you can't put it down, even if the clock is chiming midnight. You love trying to solve the mystery right along with the amateur sleuth who's in the midst of some serious detective work.

Now escape with brand-new cozy mysteries from *Heartsong Presents—MYSTERIES!* Each one is guaranteed to challenge your mind, warm your heart, touch your spirit—and put your sleuthing skills to the ultimate test. These are charming mysteries, filled with tantalizing plots and multifaceted (and often quirky) characters, but with satisfying endings that make sense.

Each cozy mystery is approximately 250 pages long, engaging your puzzle-solving abilities from the opening pages. Reading these new lighthearted, inspirational mysteries, you'll find out "whodunit" without all the gore and violence. And you'll love the romantic thread that runs through each book, too!

**Look forward to receiving mysteries like this on a regular basis—
join today and receive 4 FREE books with your
first 4 book club selections!**

As a member of the *Heartsong Presents—Mysteries! Book Club*, four of the newest releases in cozy, contemporary, full-length mysteries will be delivered to your door every six weeks for the low price of $13.99. *And shipping and handling is FREE!*

- -

YES! Sign me up for **Heartsong Presents—MYSTERIES!**

NEW MEMBERSHIPS WILL BE SHIPPED IMMEDIATELY!
Send no money now. We'll bill you only $13.99 postpaid with your first shipment of four books. Or for faster action, call 1-740-922-7280.

NAME _____

ADDRESS_____

CITY_____ ST_____ ZIP_____

**Mail to: HEARTSONG MYSTERIES,
PO Box 721, Uhrichsville, Ohio 44683
Or sign up at WWW.HEARTSONGMYSTERIES.COM**